AMY REDEK

Loving
THE MECHANIC

HOT BI-SEXUAL EROTICA

WARNING

This book contains sexually explicit scenes and adult language. It may be considered offensive to some readers. This book is for sale to adults ONLY.

* * * * * * * * * * * * * * * * * * *

Please store your files wisely where they cannot be accessed by underage readers.

Please feel free to send me an email. Just know that these emails are filtered by my publisher. Good news is always welcome.

Amy Redek – **amy_redek@awesomeauthors.org**

You might also want to check my blog for Updates and interesting info. http://amy-redek.awesomeauthors.org/

About the Publisher

4Fun Publishing, a member of **BLVNP Incorporated**, 340 S. Lemon #6200, Walnut CA 91789, info@blvnp.com / legal@blvnp.com

NOTE: Due to the highly emotional reaction of some people to works of erotic fiction, any email sent to the above address that contains foul language or religious references is automatically deleted by our anti-spam software and will not be seen. All other communications are welcome.

DISCLAIMER

Please don't be stupid and kill yourself. This book is a work of FICTION. Do not try any new sexual practice that you find in this book. It is fiction and not to be confused with reality. Neither the author nor the publisher or its associates assume any responsibility for any loss, injury, death or legal consequences resulting from acting on the contents in this book. Every character in this book is over 18 years of age. The author's opinions are not to be construed as the opinions of the publisher. The material in this book is for entertainment purposes ONLY. Enjoy.

Loving the Mechanic
Hot Bi-Sexual Erotica

By: Amy Redek

© Amy Redek 2014
ISBN: 978-1-62761-829-8

THE ONLY thing I had to remind me of my parents was a few photographs. They were killed in a road accident when I was just a toddler, and it was my uncle and aunt who raised me. A good job they did too, especially with my education.

The car accident that my parents had been involved in made me want to know everything there was to know about motor vehicles of all types. Not wanting to be a simple mechanic and tie myself to just being a garage hand, I decided that the best place to learn was in the army. The REME's to be precise.

So I knuckled down to do my studying, having found out the requirements to join this part of the armed forces, the G.C.S.E.'s and the grades required. When I reached the age of eighteen, I then applied to join the army and was taken on and became a Vehicle Mechanic B (VM(B)). Mind you, I still had to go through all the training to become a soldier on top of spending twenty weeks in my mechanical training, which I passed quite high in, and spent two years in Germany and three in the Middle East.

Even though I was in areas of military combat, I didn't have cause to become involved in any of the fighting, just seeing that the vehicles used were in tip top condition. Whilst in Germany, I was promoted to corporal and out in the deserts of Iraq and Iran, was made up to a sergeant. But after five years of this and now fully qualified in being able to service and repair all kinds of vehicles and having the licence to drive up to the biggest that can be driven on the roads, I decided to leave the army and find the work I was now qualified to do.

Having always spent my leave at my uncle and aunt's home where I was brought up, I decided that I would move out and find a good firm to work for, which could be anywhere in the country. I was now twenty-three years old and it was time to flee the nest. This I did, but still stayed in contact with them, sending them birthday and Christmas cards and the odd visits over the coming years.

With my army pay being saved over the years, I was now free to roam the country having listed all the major haulage firms, checking them out. It was three weeks after I'd started looking at those listed that I came across Webb's Haulage, a family run business in the Midlands.

Here I got lucky, for one of their drivers had just cracked some bones in his leg and was hospitalised. He had just returned from a trip to Germany and on getting out of the cab, had fallen and done the damage to his leg which meant he was out of action for at least three months. After the owner, Graham Webb, the father of the firm, looked through my credentials, he took me on immediately. Not only to do the regular run to Germany, my having learned to speak the language as well, but also to service the other trucks that they had instead of having to pay the firm they usually used in doing this.

Their yard and house, which was on the premises, was out on the edge of town and so I found myself some lodgings in town and would have to take a bus to get there in the mornings. It would be a few days before the next run to Germany, so I got to know the Webb family members.

Graham Webb, the owner, looked after the foreign contracts. His eldest son Michael, thirty years of age, looked after the England contracts and was married to Sheila, who looked after the house with the wife of Graham having died some years before. The second son, Peter, twenty-eight years old, was in charge of the drivers. He had two daughters, Katherine, twenty-five years old, was known as Katie and ran the household and was helped in the kitchen by Sheila. Katie also looked after the canteen and was sometimes helped out by the younger daughter called Samantha, though she preferred to be called Sam, who was the same age as myself.

The day came round for my first run to Germany, this truck doing the journey twice a month, taking a whole week there and back, sleeping in the cab which had a fold down bed behind the driver's seat. The day before this first trip for me, I gave the truck an overhaul and was satisfied that it was road worthy and was given enough money to buy fuel on the journey. I didn't have to pay the ferry for this was done on a contract basis and paid direct from the office.

So early the next morning, I took the truck out to call on two firms to load the truck for me to deliver to two other firms in Hamburg and Cologne, known as Koln in Germany. I had been given maps of where to collect from and the places for delivery.

With the collections being made, it was then down to Dover for the ferry crossing, my slot having already been booked. We landed in France that evening, where I then had my sleep. The times of my stopping had to be observed because of the tachograph, (the name used by drivers which really was named as being a tachometer), which registered the times that the vehicle was in motion and the speed, having to follow the rules laid down by law.

I soon made the deliveries, only having to ask once in each town exactly where it was that I had to deliver to, before then making my way to Amsterdam in Holland to collect some goods for delivery in England. Then it was off to catch the ferry at Calais to deliver what I had collected and was back in our depot exactly a week after departure.

Graham called me into his office and congratulated me on my first trip without having had any problems. As there wouldn't be a Germany run for another two weeks, he expected me to check over the other six vehicles and be prepared to take another truck out if some other driver failed to turn up for work. This I understood and went off and caught a bus to drop me off near the place that I had lodgings in.

With the next day being a Saturday, having this day off and the Sunday, I strolled around the town to have my meals and find a decent pub to have a beer in. On the Sunday, I went and saw a movie before stopping off at a pub later for a meal and a pint.

On Monday, I was laying on a small trolley beneath a truck when I had my foot kicked. I propelled out from under and looked up to see that it was Sam who had kicked my foot.

'How was your first trip, Eddie?' she asked, looking down at me. I forgot to tell you that my name really was Edward. Edward Arthur May was the name I was given when christened, but had always been called Eddie. This was the second time I had seen Sam, the first being in the canteen. Back then she had then been wearing an overall, but now without it, I could clearly see that she had a really nice figure, being rather big on top and narrow at the waist, coupled with a lovely smile. Still lying on my back on the trolley, I could see quite clearly that she was wearing white panties and had nice, slender legs.

'Fine, Sam. Just fine,' I replied. I could see that her eyes were running up and down my body as I had looked at hers. Being underneath the truck, I had taken off my T shirt and I was wearing a pair of cut down jeans. That's having cut the legs off to make them like shorts.

'You've got a nice physique, Eddie,' she said with a smile, which was true having really kept myself fit whilst in the army.

'I can say the same for you, Sam,' I replied, giving her a smile back.

'It's tea break in ten minutes. I thought you ought to know,' she said.

'I'd prefer coffee if it's possible,' I replied, sitting up with my legs now astride of the trolley. I saw her eyes look down at my groin and felt myself getting hard inside the tight shorts at the smile she gave me, which I'm sure she noticed.

'I can do that for you,' she said, the tip of her tongue coming out from her mouth and moving across her lips. Her eyes were bright and shining and I wondered if she could do more for me too. I wasn't a virgin when it came to sex, having had a few girlfriends when I was stationed out in Germany, and wondered if there was a chance of bedding her.

'See you in the canteen then,' she said before turning away and walking off to where the canteen was with me watching the way her bum moved from side to side as she walked away.

I got up from the trolley and went off to the toilets where I could wash my hands and went into one of the cubicles and pulled out my erection that she had caused and jerked myself off, sending my cum into the toilet bowl. When it was back to its normal state, I went off to the canteen where there were a couple of other guys having their tea and a bun, or something like that to eat, and got my coffee from Sam, declining the snack offered. I took my coffee and went and joined the other two men in there and introduced myself. They had the advantage of already knowing my name and told me theirs. One, Roger, it was his truck I was servicing, asked if it would be ready by lunchtime for he had an afternoon run. I assured him it would be ready by then.

We made small talk for the fifteen-minute break, them wanting to know what it had been like in the army, noting my chest and arms being muscular without me wearing a shirt like they were, and were quite impressed at what I told them, or so I liked to think.

With the break over, I was back under the truck and finally passed it as roadworthy for Roger to then take it over to do his run. The other guy, Brian, had already left the yard and so I was the only one in the canteen for lunch that was served up to me by Sam. She also got herself something to eat and sat down with me. She wanted to know all the ins and outs of what I had been doing before coming to work for her dad. So for the whole hour of my lunch break, I told her of life in the army. Only getting back a little information about herself which wasn't much.

I DID another three runs to Germany without any problems and we were expecting Steve, the driver who had splintered his leg falling out of the truck I was driving, back within a couple of weeks. I was in the yard cleaning out the cab of my truck, it being late afternoon, when Peter came out into the yard and called me over.

'Come with me into town,' he began. 'Brian's had an accident.'

I followed him to his car and got in and he drove us off to the police station. That was our destination as Brian was there and on the way, he told me what he knew so far. 'Brian had just started to cross the main road with the green light when a motor cyclist tried to jump the red one on his side. He tried to swerve to miss Brian, but skidded and he and the bike collided with the underside of the truck. He must have damaged the fuel tank for they had to tow the truck off to the side of the road and have a fire engine spray the road to clear away the diesel that had come out of the tank. That's all I know at the moment.'

It wasn't long before we arrived at the police station, having passed our truck to where it had been towed. Brian had been breathalysed and they had taken his tachograph out of the cab. He passed the test and the taco was okay in respect of his driving time and speed of the truck when he moved off with having the green light. The police had witness reports to say that cleared Brian as it was the fault of the motor cyclist that resulted in the collision. They gave Peter the details of the cyclist, who had been taken to the hospital with cuts and bruises for him to claim the insurance, plus the tachograph disc and keys to the truck, and with Brian, left the police station.

We stopped where the truck was parked and I went underneath to inspect the damage and found that the tank was still leaking diesel and that the connecting pipe had broken away from the tank.

'I can't fix it here,' I told Peter when I pulled myself out from underneath the truck. 'It'll have to be towed to the yard.' Peter nodded and used his mobile phone to call up a towing agency and we waited till the tow truck arrived and it wasn't long before the front wheels were off the ground with the front chained and hauled up. With the truck being towed away, we followed it to the yard when it finished up, now being home for me to see to repairing the damage.

We'd been away for over three hours and it was just coming up to nightfall, so I got some lights out into the yard and placed them on the ground so that I could properly inspect the damage. The first thing was to put a can beneath the tank and drained it of what fuel was left inside. Then I got the steam cleaning equipment out and really cleaned out the tank and where some fuel had spread on the ground. As I was going to use some welding equipment, I didn't want the bloody thing catching fire. I had to cut away the damaged bracket first to replace it later and saw to sealing the tank first before I could do this.

With the tank now okay with it being sealed and a new bracket fitted, I broke off working as I was given something to eat in the canteen as it was now well past dinner time. After that, it was to fix the new piece of pipe into place that fed the engine. With this in place, I siphoned some fuel into the tank and managed to get the engine started. I let it run for a little while, checking underneath to see that the seams of the tank were not leaking and then drove the truck over to where the fuel pump was and filled the tank.

Brian had been sent home just after our arrival at the yard as there was no point in him hanging around. Peter had brought me out some coffee before I had finished and with it all now done and the truck fit and ready for the next day's run, I found that it was well past midnight. Graham, Katie and Sam had come out into the yard when we had first gotten the truck in but had now all gone to bed.

'You look absolutely filthy,' said Peter when I had finished. 'You need a good shower. And as it's late, you might as well sleep here for the night. Come.' He beckoned me to follow him to the big house where the family lived.

It really was big, having been built in Queen Victoria's time. The hall light was still on as well as the inside light for the stairs that led up to their bedrooms. I followed him up and into his bedroom where, some years earlier, he told me, all the bedrooms had had separate bathrooms installed. He took me into what was a large bathroom having not only the usual things there, but a big shower too. He turned this on and watched as I took my dirty clothes off, not fit for wearing now without being washed, and got under the hot water and washed myself with him there the whole time.

With me being clean, I got out of the shower where he handed me a big towel to dry myself and wrapping it round my waist when done, followed him back into the bedroom.

'You don't mind sleeping in the same bed with me?' he asked, to which I said I didn't, having had to sleep with other guys when out in the desert. 'Sleep on the right,' he said as he began to take his clothes off while I had only the towel to take off and got into bed and watched him, now being as naked as I was, get into the bed alongside me. 'I'll let you have some of my clothes in the morning as yours are not fit to wear now until they've been cleaned. You've done a good bit of repairing the truck which dad will thank you for in the morning,' he said. With that, he turned off the bedside lamp and we settled down to sleep.

It was a few minutes later, me lying on my left side when his body came up against mine. I felt his naked body nestle up against me. His right hand began to stroke me from the armpit down to my thigh.

'You've got a nice strong body, Eddie,' he whispered as he stroked me and I wasn't really surprised when his hand came over my thigh from the stroking and taking hold of my cock which had started to rise up with what his hand had been doing. 'A nice big cock too,' he added, as his fingers curled round the shaft and began rubbing his hand up and down, making it rise up into a full erection. He did this for a minute or two, giving me a thrill of having his hand holding it in a firm grip before he spoke again. 'Have you ever had this sucked before?'

'Once,' I replied, my voice quite croaky.

'Man or woman?' he asked.

'A woman,' I replied.

'Well it's such a lovely cock, would you let me suck on it and be the first man to do so?'

I didn't know what to say, and with me not saying anything, he took my silence to be a yes, for he moved his body back away from me and still holding my hard and throbbing cock in his hand, pulled me over onto my back. His hand still holding me fast and moving it up and down as I felt him move further down the bed and under the covers. I felt his cheek slide down over my stomach and felt his hot breath over the head of my cock as he eased the foreskin right down and had him take it into his mouth.

Boy, that was hot. I couldn't help the gasp that I gave out at having my cock for the second time being taken into a mouth that seemed on fire it was that hot. My body trembled and twitched as his tongue moved over the bare flesh, touching the G string, giving me a thrilling tingle that moved up and down my spine. His head began bobbing up and down in an opposite motion to his hand, really giving me a thrill at my not using my own hand in jerking myself off. I could feel his saliva coating the head making it easier to move in his mouth, his lips tight just under the head and gave out a groan at the pleasure he was giving me. So much so, that I wasn't far off cumming.

'I'm going to cum,' I gasped at feeling the suction as well as his tongue roving round the bare flesh.

'I know,' he said, briefly lifting his head up off of my cock. 'Let it go for me to taste.' He took it back into his mouth to continue sucking, his hand gripping me tight and moving a bit faster in moving it up and down.

The cheeks of my bum tightened and began to slightly lift my hips up towards him as I felt my cum starting its journey up to oblivion, finally erupting into his mouth, giving him at least six shots. Being empty, my body then relaxed as I felt my cum being moved over and round the head of my cock with his tongue and then that extra pressure as he sucked it up into his throat for him to swallow. He carried on using his tongue to sweep over and round the head, cleaning it up before lifting his head up and giving it a kiss before moving back up in the bed, his hand still slowly moving up and down the slowly deflating cock of mine.

'You taste lovely Eddie,' he whispered, kissing the side of my neck, his breath hot against my skin. 'Will you let me do it again in the morning?'

'Ye…yes,' I stammered. 'It was better than that woman did.'

'Lovely,' he crooned, his hand now leaving my cock that was now only half as hard as it had been a few minutes ago, and began stroking my chest as he cuddled up close to me. I could feel his erection pressing up against my thigh, and hoped that he didn't ask me to suck on him, which he didn't. We both fell asleep.

I CAME awake with him back down the bed and sucking on my morning erection.

I gave out a groan at the pleasure he was giving me, letting him know that I was coming awake. With his hand firmly moving the soft skin up and down over the hard piece of flesh, I gave up the cum that had accumulated during the night. Again I felt the suction as he swallowed it and had him licking the head clean before releasing me to come back up from under the covers and giving me a kiss on the cheek.

'It tasted even better than last night,' he said. 'Let's have a shower and get dressed for breakfast.' With that, he let go of me and rolled over and got out of bed, his cock sticking out from his groin. I got out too, and followed him into the bathroom. I watched the cheeks of his bum moving about as I walked behind him, wondering what it would be like pushing my cock up in between them. He turned on the shower before pushing me inside and him following, with there being enough room for the two of us.

There was a soap dispenser fitted to the wall and he squirted some soap out into his hand and began to wash my cock and balls for me. I leaned back against the tiled wall as he did so.

'Will you wash mine now?' he asked when he'd finished, and I looked down to see that he still had this erection. I moved forward to do as he asked; it was the least I could do. With soap on my hand, I began to wash his cock and balls.

'Will you jerk me off too?' he asked, and so turning him round, I moved up tight to his body, feeling my cock being squashed against the cheeks of his bum as I held him round the waist with my left hand as I began to jerk him off with my right. He leaned back towards me, wriggling his bum against my cock as I moved my hand up and down his cock until I felt his body stiffen and felt his cum moving up the tube of his cock and had it shoot out to hit the tiled wall, it slowly being washed down with the spraying water.

'I needed that,' he said when he'd finished and with that, he turned the water off and got out of the shower and got two towels out of the cupboard there for us to dry ourselves. When done, we went back into the bedroom where he rummaged through a chest of drawers and the wardrobe and got out some clothes for me to wear.

There were surprised looks on the faces of the family when I walked into the dining room with Peter, who then told them why I was there.

'Another one to feed, Sheila,' he said, her being the wife of Michael. 'Eddie worked till well past midnight in getting the truck repaired fit to be used today,' he said, speaking to his father. 'The least I could do was let him sleep over as the bus had stopped running by then. Plus he needed a shower and his clothes were filthy, so I've lent him some of mine.'

'So the truck's okay then?' Graham asked me as I was pushed into a chair by Peter. 'The tank looked a mess last night.'

'Well it will do until we get a new one,' I replied. 'I don't know how long it will last but it's roadworthy, that I can assure you.'

I thanked Sheila for the big plate of eggs, sausages and bacon that had been placed in front of me. I was so hungry that I wanted to wolf it down but remembered my manners and took it easy. I still cleared the plate and had a slice of buttered toast and washed it all down with two cups of coffee, though.

I thanked Sheila and Katie as well as Graham for letting me dine with them and gave them my apologies for not offering to help with the washing up as I had work to do. I think that this went down well with the boss as he left the table with me and followed me out and into the yard where he inspected the work I had done last evening.

He agreed in getting a new fuel tank but suggested that the old one was left on till the new one was needed. I was quite pleased with myself at doing a good job in getting that truck back out onto the road. Brian was pleased too with what I had done. So was Sam, that is, until tea break. She had made me coffee and sat down with me in the canteen.

'How was the bed last night?' she asked.

'Fine,' I said.

'But surely the sheets were damp. That spare room hasn't been used for ages,' she said.

'I beg your pardon. Spare room?' I asked, somewhat bewildered.

'Yes, the spare room. Did Peter change the sheets for you?'

'No,' I told her, 'I slept in his bed.'

'What!' she cried out. 'Didn't you know he is gay?'

'Not at the time, but I do now,' I grinned.

'Don't tell me you fucked him and had him fuck you?' she demanded with a sour look on her face.

'No!' I exclaimed.

'You didn't have sex with him then?' she asked, the expression on her face almost back to normal.

'Er, well, sort of,' I admitted. I had been brought up to not tell lies. It's easy to remember the truth but difficult to remember lies.

'What do you mean sort of?' she demanded, her eyes now flashing and giving out danger signals.

'Well, er, he sort of sucked on me,' I said somewhat chastely, looking down at my coffee cup and not looking her in the eye.

'So you then went and sucked on his cock?' she exclaimed, almost shouting now.

'No! I didn't,' I cried back, now facing her but refrained from saying that I jerked him off in the shower. Least said, least mended was my excuse.

'Well that's something I suppose,' she said. 'I really should have warned you that he was gay,' she said.

I let it drop for the time being for I would later in the week, ask her out to the cinema and I would then find out.

'Time I was back to work,' I said. 'Thanks for the coffee.'

NOW MY official working hours were from eight in the morning till five in the afternoon, but didn't leave at that time if a truck was late returning to the yard. I didn't claim overtime when this happened, like I didn't ask when I worked on Brian's truck until after midnight. Well on the Thursday afternoon, Roger phoned in from his mobile that he was caught up in a traffic hold-up on the motorway and would be late.

I was told this at five o'clock and so I stayed on with all the other trucks in and the drivers having gone home. I sat in the canteen drinking coffee with Peter until Roger finally drove into the yard. The reason I stayed on, was to give his truck a quick run through to see that it was okay to be out on the road the following day. Roger apologised for delaying me to do my check, but I waved him away and got on with looking it over.

With this done, I told Peter that it was fine and he then surprised me by saying that he would drive me home after staying on late. Well I didn't refuse and got into his car and gave him the address where I was lodging.

'Would you like to come in for a beer?' I asked him, being polite with the offer after having him drive me home, such as it was. This he accepted and I led him up to the room I was renting and got us both a can of beer out of the fridge.

'Some bloody dump,' he remarked, swigging at the can having refused a glass. I had to agree with him, the place only having a miniscule kitchen, a small sitting room and a smaller bedroom. The bathroom and toilet, which I had to share with others, was down the hall.

'I've lived in worse places than this in the past,' I said sitting down next to him on the dilapidated sofa, gulping down some of my beer.

'You know,' he began after a minute or two of silence, 'I liked that cock of yours. The biggest I've ever sucked on. Would...would you use it to fuck me?' he asked.

I should say that I was dumbfounded at him asking me this, but somehow, I knew that he would eventually want me to have some sort of sex with him. I just didn't expect it so soon after our night in bed together.

'I…I don't know what to say, Peter,' I told him. 'Besides, I haven't got any condoms.'

'I have,' he replied with a grin. 'I always carry a few with me all the time with the prospect of using them sometime. Will you let me have your lovely cock up inside me?'

Now this would be another first for me, but as he'd already sucked on me, why not, I said to myself, my cock already reacting to his question and telling me that it would be okay.

'Er, well, if you want me to,' I said rather lamely. 'It's a lousy bed that I've got here.'

'We can do it here. On the carpet,' he answered, his eyes shining at the prospect.

'Ok….okay,' I stammered, wondering what it would be like.

'Great,' he exclaimed, putting his beer can down on the floor and standing up to peel off his trousers, letting me see his cock, smaller than mine I must say, and pulling a condom out of his trousers before throwing them on the sofa. I too put my beer can down and stood up and got my trousers off for him to see that my cock was up and rampant.

'Looks good enough to eat,' he said as he went down onto his knees. Taking hold of my cock, he opened his mouth and took the head inside.

I gasped at the heat of his lips. After pushing the foreskin down, he ran his tongue over the bare flesh, making my body shudder. It was only for a brief time that he did this before letting go of it to sit back onto his heels to rip the condom packet open and pull out the rubber and then roll it down over my still hard and throbbing cock.

'There,' he said, beginning to turn round on his knees to show me his backside. 'You shouldn't need telling where it's got to go, Eddie.'

I looked at the bum cheeks that I had seen a couple of days ago and so here I was having it offered to me and slowly got between his open legs and went down onto my knees and in between them. Seeing his puckered ring piece made me wonder if my cock would fit inside it, but there must be some give in it for he crapped as any other human and animal did.

I put my left hand up onto his thigh as I held my cock in the other and shuffled further forward and put the covered head to the entrance of his ass. I felt his body tremble as it touched his ring piece and using my body weight to hold it there, let go of my cock and put my hand onto his other hips and leaned my body forward.

I watched as I felt the resistance give, and the head of my cock slowly disappeared into his ass. He give out some grunts until the head slipped in to be followed by as much of the shaft that his bum cheeks would allow. Christ! His ass was as hot as his mouth had been and instead of feeling his tongue, it was his sphincter muscle that kept flexing itself round my shaft. He had given out a gasp as I had widened his ass hole and now he began to croon as I moved myself backwards and forwards in this first time of fucking ass. It was tighter than a female's pussy, giving me more feeling. I began to enjoy fucking him.

My cock must have liked where it was for it wasn't long before my hands were gripping his thighs tighter and pulled his body back onto my throbbing cock as I began to shoot my load, albeit into a condom, until I came to a panting stop and leaned over his rear end. My cock was still throbbing away inside him as his muscle kept up its rhythmic flexing.

'Fucking lovely Eddie,' Peter got out in gasps. 'The best yet.'

I straightened up, now having cummed, and my breathing almost back to normal. I pulled out to Peter's cries of, what I found out later, dismay at losing what had given him pleasure. Well I was quite pleased with myself too, for having the nerve to actually fuck another man up the ass.

Out I came and sat back on my heels for a moment, but Peter was quicker in his turning round and pulling the condom off of me and then taking the still hard cock head into his mouth to try and suck out any remains of my cum as well as licking off that which still covered the head. When he finally released me, he looked up with a big smile on his face as he licked his lips.

'Man! That was some fuck! The best yet,' he cried, his eyes shining up at me. 'What say you?' he asked in that old English way.

'I agree. It was much better than I thought it would be,' I told him as I got up from the floor and began to put my trousers back on. It seemed to be with some reluctance that he got up himself and put his own trousers on.

'I'd better be going home or they will start wondering why I was away so long,' he said in a shy voice. Me wanting him to go too though I told him to finish his beer first. This we both did before putting the empty cans down and went over to the door where he turned round and startled me by kissing me on the lips. 'Thanks, Eddie. Maybe we can do this again some night. See you tomorrow.' With that, he left.

My mind was in turmoil as I went into my bedroom, having just fucked my first male person up the ass, the main problem being that I had enjoyed it. Enjoyed it nearly as much as when he had sucked on me. But it was Sam that I wanted. I wanted her to prove that I really was a man and not like Peter in pretending to be a woman by wanting another man instead. In spite of the ranging thoughts of my mind, I still jerked myself off when I was in bed reliving the pleasure I had got by having Peter.

I WAS at work on time the next day and it wasn't until lunch that I asked Sam if she would let me take her to the pictures that evening. I even threw in that we could have dinner out as well.

'I'd like that,' she said with a coy smile. 'What time?'

'Well, to save me travelling back and forth, why not come with me when we close down for the night. I can then change into something decent and we can have a meal and then the cinema. How's that?' I said.

'Fine by me,' she said with that lovely smile on her face. So when the last truck came in, I had checked over them all by five and found that Sam was dressed, ready and waiting for me. She looked stunning in the skirt and blouse and took my arm as we left the yard to go and catch the bus into town.

I was somewhat ashamed of taking her into the room I rented, more so at her exclamation on entering it. 'You're living in this dump?'

'Well the rent is cheap,' I said contritely.

'Cheap? They should pay you to live here.'

'I'm sorry, but it's all I could find here in town,' I told her in an apologetic way.

'Hrummph,' was the snorting retort I got as I left her in the sitting room to change into the only decent set of clothes I had. This didn't take long and we soon left my room to go to the only decent restaurant in town and had an early dinner.

We might have started early but were there for well over an hour having a lovely meal and drinking two bottles of wine between us. She wanted to know more of my army life and that took up most of the time.

'What were the women like when you were out in the Middle East?' was one of the more pertinent questions I got from her.

'Untouchable. You daren't even speak to one out there for you would more likely to be attacked and have your balls cut off. Oh, sorry. I shouldn't have said that last bit,' I said blushing.

'Well you wouldn't then be any threat to them having that done,' she laughed.

That really was the only thing of note that we spoke of while having our dinner. After paying for the meal, I escorted her to the cinema where I bought the tickets and some kind of popcorn before we were shown where we could sit.

It was nice to sit there in the darkness as the film played its way. It soon bored me and I put my arm round her shoulder and pulled her towards me and kissed her. There wasn't any resistance and so I carried on kissing her and she didn't stop my hand from working its way inside her blouse to find that she wasn't wearing a bra. It was lovely to be able to take that ample sized breast into my hand and gently mould it as we kissed, feeling the nipple rise up to be as hard as a nut.

What made the evening more thrilling was while we were kissing and with me fondling her tits, I felt her hand start to rub the front of my trousers, feeling that I was as hard as an iron bar. I don't know how I managed to control myself by not cumming inside them.

The popcorn wasn't eaten.

In a way, I was glad when the film came to an end for I don't think I could have lasted much longer with the way she was stroking me through my trousers without me cumming. Just before the cinema theatre's lights came on, my hand was out of her blouse and she had it buttoned up so that we didn't have to fumble with our clothes where everybody could have seen us doing so. We left the cinema with everybody else and I suggested one more drink before I took her home, to which she agreed. So we went into the bar near the bus stop where I had a beer and she had a sherry.

These were finished in time to catch the bus which stopped about a hundred yards from the yard, were we then walked hand in hand and stopped just outside of the gates for us to hold and kiss each other. This we did for several minutes before we broke apart and I looked at my watch. It had gone past eleven o'clock.

'Shit! I've missed the last bus,' I said. This being the bus we had got off from the town, me not realising then that it only had two more stops from where we got off before it turned round and began its last run back to town. 'It's nearly two bloody miles.'

'Never mind,' she said. 'Come inside, for I've got an idea.'

What it was, she wouldn't tell me outside, so I followed her inside the yard, locking the gate behind us before going to the big house at the back. We still held hands until we reached the house and she used a key to get in, beckoning me inside too. We went into the lounge where Graham, her father was sitting down reading a newspaper.

'You're late,' he said looking up as we entered.

'Yes, but we didn't realise that the bus was the last one so Eddie has missed it. Can I fix up the spare room for the night and he can catch one in the morning?' she asked of her father.

'Of course,' he replied and she gave me a smile and disappeared upstairs.

'Sit down Eddie,' Graham said. 'Fancy a nightcap?' he asked as I sat myself down.

'Eh, yes please,' I replied.

'Gin, whisky, vodka?' was the question he asked.

'Er, vodka and tonic if you don't mind.'

'No problem,' he said and poured the drinks into two glasses and brought them over and handed me one as he sat down.

'What film did you see?' he asked. That floored me.

'I-I can't remember what it was called,' I said shamefaced.

'I'm not surprised with you being with Sam,' he chortled. 'Well it looks like that next week's run to Germany will be the last for a time as we expect Steve back sometime next week. You did a fine job with that as well as what you've been doing with the trucks. So much so, that I've decided to get another four later for you to look after. I'm getting more collect and delivery orders than we can handle at the moment so with you now being here to look after them, I think it's about time we expanded. It'll be more work for you so I will be upping your wages.'

'Er, thank you sir,' I said, pleased that I was now accepted as being a good worker.

'Eddie. Out in the yard, "sir" is the right response, but here at home, it's Graham. Understand?'

'Er, yes si…Graham, and thank you.' At which point, Sam came back into the lounge.

'We'll talk a bit more about this tomorrow,' he said.

'Drinks?' Sam said. 'Can I have one too?'

'Yes,' Graham said, 'and two fresh Vodka and tonics for us. I've just promoted Eddie.' Now that was news to me not realising that this was intended.

'That's great, daddy, for he deserves it,' she said as she poured out a drink for herself as well as another two for us.

'What film did you see tonight?' he asked her.

'Er, I can't remember what it was called,' she answered him and it made him chuckle again, giving me a wink, and I'm sure the bastard knew exactly why neither of us could name the film. 'Why the promotion for Eddie?' she asked him as she sat down between us on the sofa.

'Well he's going to have to handle four more trucks that Michael and I have decided to buy. We're getting more orders than we can handle with what we've got, so it's new trucks and new drivers. It'll take a week or two before we get them and then we'll advertise for drivers for them,' he told her.

'That's wonderful, daddy. I'm sure that Eddie can handle them,' she gushed and I saw the look in his eyes and wondered what he'd read in her remark regarding me. They talked more between them and it appeared that at least two of them would be out on runs to Europe.

'Oh, there's one other thing Eddie,' he began, addressing me. 'We're also getting a small truck for you to stock up with relevant parts in case of a breakdown, or, God forbid, an accident to one of those out on the road, so that you can go out and get it back to us without getting, and paying some other haulage company to bring it home. I just hope that it will not really be used for that for a long time yet, but it's just to be on the safe side.'

'That's a good idea si...er, Graham,' I replied, finishing my drink. Sam noticed that I had done so and quickly swallowed hers. She then took my empty glass from me and put both on the side of the dresser where the drinks were held.

'Time for bed. I'll leave a note for Sheila that there's an extra one for breakfast,' she said to Graham and beckoned me to follow her upstairs.

'Thanks for the drink, Graham, and letting me stay the night.'

'You're welcome,' was the reply before I left the lounge to follow Sam.

Up the stairs we went and she stopped at a door just past that of Peter's and opened the door and led me in.

'I've changed the sheets, giving you fresh ones and put some towels into the bathroom there,' pointing at that door. She then came over to me and gave me a kiss. 'Don't go out and into Peter's room,' she said before she left me there in my room for the night. I found out the reason for that remark a little later.

I HAD a shower after she had left, to cool myself down, and it was nice to be in a room by myself that was much bigger and comfortable than the dingy room of where I lodged. The sheets were nice and soft and I snuggled down nicely and with the lamp turned off, relived those few hours in the cinema with Sam, getting an erection at not only feeling and rubbing her tits but also of her stroking my covered cock.

I was just on the point of falling asleep when I heard the door opening and wondered if my thoughts and dreams were about to come true. They were, for it was Sam who had entered the room and came over to the bed and got inside for our naked bodies to touch each other.

'Sam! You shouldn't be here,' I whispered.

'Why not? I've wanted us to be like this from the very first time I saw you,' she whispered back. 'What the fuck are we whispering for?' she said in her normal voice.

'Well I don't want your father to know that you are here in bed with me,' I whispered, still not wanting to be heard outside of the bedroom.

'Dad's not stupid, Eddie. He knows damn well why I wanted you to sleep here tonight. So don't worry about that. He knows that I'm not a virgin. Besides, he likes you and won't say anything, so don't have a guilty look on your face at breakfast. Now let me feel again what I felt in the cinema.' Her hand moved down from my chest and found that I was up and hard. 'Oooh, this feels lovely. Come on, Eddie! Don't just lie there. Carry on from where we left off in the cinema,' she said, her hand now moving up and down on my cock.

So I did just that, turning to face her in the dim light of the room and kissing her as my hand began to mould one of her breasts.

'If you keep on doing what you are doing Sam, I'm going to cum too soon,' I murmured and moved myself down the bed a little way, making it slip out of her hand as my lips closed round a stiff and hard nipple. It was upstanding enough for me to be able to nibble it with my teeth as well as sucking on it. My hand moved down over her flat stomach and through the soft pubic hair until my fingers were able to open the labia lips and find her clit.

She gave out a groan and a slight shudder of her body at me flicking it with that finger, but then I replaced it with my thumb so that I could then insert two fingers into her vagina and move them about, creating more groans from her as her body began to squirm.

'I'm going to cum soon with what you are doing, Eddie. Put yourself inside me and let's cum together,' she panted.

I didn't need telling twice. I moved my body over hers, her legs opening wider for me to get in between them. It was easy then to move slightly higher and kiss her as the head of my cock found the entrance to her pussy. She trembled beneath me and her arms came up round my shoulders, pulling me down onto her breasts that got squashed as I moved my cock up inside her.

'Wow. That feels great,' she gasped as our pubes met. I felt her flexing her inside muscles all round my hard cock that was inside her as far as it was going to go. She began to move in time with me as I began fucking her, my body moving up as hers moved down, her legs lifting the bed cover up, trying to get more of me inside her. It had been a couple of years since I last had a woman beneath me and I tried to hold on longer, but couldn't. I was soon up to ramming speed and began to shudder on top of her as I unloaded my cum up in to the hot oven that encompassed my throbbing cock.

'Oh Eddie, darling! I can feel it!' she gasped. Her muscles squeezing me as hard as she could, virtually forcing my cum out of my cock. I could feel her heart hammering away inside her chest as I came to a full stop, my cock now twitching inside her. 'Don't stop moving, Eddie, I'm nearly there,' she panted, moving even faster beneath me until, with her fingers digging into my shoulders, she heaved herself upwards, arching her back as her body gave out an enormous shudder as she had her orgasm.

'That's a first in a long time,' she breathed out as her body became slack as she settled back down on the bed, her muscles still squeezing me as it continued throbbing away inside her. 'Let me copy Peter by sucking on that lovely weapon you've got,' she said, her hands releasing their grip on my shoulders as I lifted my hips up and felt my cock sliding out from that hot oven of her insides. I flopped over onto my back as she then disappeared under the covers and had her hand take hold of my still hard and erect cock and gasped as she took the head into her mouth to start sucking out any leftover cum as well as licking her own juices off of it at the same time. But not only sucking on my cock, her other hand was fondling my balls at the same time. This she did for several minutes before releasing me to slither up my body to lay on top of me as she gave me a wet kiss.

'You're a wonderful man,' she said.

'And you're one hell of a woman,' I replied, now having my arms round her back and having her lovely breasts up tight to my chest.

'How long before you're up and ready again?' she asked, giving me another kiss.

'About an hour. Shouldn't you be going off to your bed?'

'Oh no! I'm staying here for you to fuck me again,' she said, moving her chest against mine, her hard nipples almost scratching me.

'What would your father say with you being in bed with me?' I asked.

'Atta girl,' she giggled.

'And what would he say about me?'

'Lucky sod,' grinning at me and giving me a kiss on the nose. 'Will you use your fingers again, for it was nice,' she said, rolling over and pulling me to be on top of her again.

I had to smile and moved down and onto my side so that I could suck and nibble at the hard nipple of the tit nearest to me as my hand stroked its way down to have my fingers once again play inside her pussy. She gave out a groan and wiggled her body as if to make herself comfortable as my thumb rubbed her clit while the two fingers moved about in her vagina. She had opened her legs as far as she could, and let me play with her for several minutes before speaking again.

'Will you use your tongue,' she begged.

Well it's something that I'd never done before, but as she had sucked on me, why not do as she asked? I let go of that nipple and kissed my way down her lower chest and over her stomach before getting myself down in between her wide open legs. For the first time, I kissed her other lips and poked my tongue in between them. I found this rather awkward and so managed to get my arms under and over her thighs to be able to use my fingers to hold these thick lips open and get my tongue further inside her.

Her body gave out a shiver and her a groan as my tongue fully rasped that hard nodule that was her equivalence of a penis and could feel the wetness of her pussy against my chin. I also stuck my tongue into her vagina to wiggle it about, get a taste of her juices in between flicking my tongue back and forth between her vagina and clit. I did this for several minutes before I felt her body start to stiffen up and her thighs trying to squash my head.

'I'm cumming,' she gurgled and began to bounce her hips upwards, her thighs tightening themselves against my shoulders. If they hadn't been between her legs, she would had suffocated me as she began to buck herself upwards and give out a small scream as she had an orgasm. The juices of this came down to my mouth and I couldn't help but take some of it into my mouth and have it slide down my throat, almost making me choke. There was more fluidity to her cumming than that of mine and I found it quite pleasant to taste as my tongue still worked away at the vagina and clit until she slumped back on the bed, now having had her second release.

I found that having successfully given her this form of sex, my cock was now up hard against my stomach and being squashed down on the lower bed sheet and beginning to hurt. So I pulled my arms from under her thighs and kissed my way back up her body, wiping my wet chin along the way until I was back on top of her with the head of my cock now probing the wet entrance of her pussy.

'Yes, yes, yes, Eddie. Put it in and give me another one,' she panted, pulling my head down to kiss me. I moved my hips for my cock to easily slide up inside her. And so I fucked her for the second time to give her a third orgasm with me only cumming twice now and got the same thrill at doing what I had wanted to do since I first saw her.

When I'd finished cumming, both of us were breathing rather heavily at the effort we had put into this joining and sharing the pleasure of having sex together. But Sam was not quite done. I was rolled over again for her to suck on me again. When she'd finished, she came back up the bed to smother me with kisses and cuddled herself to me and we both then drifted off to sleep in each other's arms.

IT WAS nice to wake up in the morning with the lovely warm body of a woman tight up to mine, feeling my hard morning erection tight up to her thighs. She woke up to my movements and rolled over onto her back and pulled me across for us to once again have sex, which gave us both the pleasure of having me cum again inside her as she had an orgasm too.

After many kisses, with me pulling out, we finally got up from the bed and both had a shower at the same time, washing each other down from the sweat both our bodies were covered in. With it now being daylight, I could see and caress the body of the woman I had fucked twice during the night and again this morning and wanted more as she had the most wonderful figure, perfectly shaped and a wonder to behold. It was rather difficult with us both trying to dry each other at the same time, but eventually manage this before leaving the bathroom for me to get dressed and her, just putting on her dressing gown and giving me a kiss before leaving the room to go and dress herself.

She was quick to do this for as I left the room I had been sleeping in, met her as she came out of hers and so we went downstairs together and into the dining room. She had left a note in the kitchen that I was staying overnight and so Sheila knew that it was an extra one for breakfast.

Graham, Michael and Peter were already sitting down as we entered and got a smile from Graham and a smirk from Michael, both of them guessing that Sam and I had had sex that night.

'Sleep well?' Graham asked of me with his face still smiling.

'Yes sir, er, Graham,' I replied. 'Er, I would like today, to work on the truck that's due for its M.O.T. on Monday, though someone else will have to take it as I'll be out early on Monday for the Germany run.'

'No problem there. You'll take it on Monday Peter, won't you?' he said to him.

'Yes dad,' he replied who had just sat down at the table having heard what I had said. Breakfast was brought in by Katie and then brought in her own as she and Sheila sat down for us all to start eating.

Afterwards, I thanked Sheila for breakfast and went out and spent the morning giving the truck a steam clean beneath and made sure that everything else about it was ready for its M.O.T. on Monday before preparing to return to my digs. That's the term used for where one was sleeping and paying rent.

I shouldn't have been surprised, when I left the locker room after cleaning myself up, to find Peter out in the yard offering to run me into town. I accepted the lift, guessing what this was going to lead to and I wasn't wrong.

'So you went and slept with Sam then,' he said to me as we drove off towards town.

'No,' I replied.

'No? Come off it. We all know that you slept together last night,' he said.

'I said no, because she came to sleep with me, not me going to sleep with her. There's a big difference in that. I didn't invite her in,' I said.

'Well you still had sex with her, didn't you?' he countered.

'Yes. What would you do if a naked woman got into your bed?' I asked.

'Kick her out. I'm not into having women. Now if it had been you, I would have made you welcome,' he said with a grin, giving me a quick glance before looking back at the road we were driving along. 'I'd love to spend the night in bed with you.'

I knew there had been an ulterior motive with him offering to drive me into town and that being that he wanted sex with me again. Now I wasn't averse to fucking him again or having him suck on me, but I was going to lay down the rules if this was the case.

'Well there's only one way we could, and that would have to be this Sunday night. You can then drive me to the yard on Monday morning for me to do the Germany run,' I said.

'Great!' he gushed. 'What time?'

'Any time after nine when I'll be in,' I said, getting a hard on at making this offer to fuck him again.

'I'll be there on time. Er, could….could we, er, have a bit of fun now?' he asked, which was what I had been expecting him to ask.

'If you like,' I told him, my cock now up really hard inside my trousers at the thought, 'though I've only got a single bed.'

'Bed, bathroom, floor, anywhere would be good,' he replied, taking a hand off the steering wheel and running it up and down my thigh, feeling that I had an erection already. 'You're ready already,' he simpered before putting his hand back onto the wheel to turn off into the road where I was staying. He parked the car and we went into the house and up to my room, and when the door was closed behind us, he put his arms round me and gave me a kiss. 'I need you as much as Sam did,' he breathed, rubbing his body tight up against mine, feeling that he had an erection too.

'We'll use the bed this time,' I said, leading the way into the small bedroom. 'I still haven't got any condoms.'

'Like a boy scout, I always come prepared,' he gave out a giggle. 'Cum being the operative word.'

He was quicker than me in getting our clothes off and was on the bed before me, his erection lying up on his stomach. Mine was sticking out in front of me and swung from side to side as I got onto the bed, him moving to one side to make room, our cocks clashing together.

'I'm going to enjoy having this again,' he said as he took hold of my cock, giving it a rub. 'It's lovely to suck on.' I then foolishly went and asked the wrong question.

'What's it like, sucking on an erect cock?' was the most stupid thing I could have asked, realising then that I had opened the door for him.

'Just great. Why not give it a try? We could both do it together at the same time,' he said, his eyes alight and having a big smile on his face. 'You might enjoy it as much as I do.'

'How do we do that?' I asked. He gave me a grin.

'Give me a kiss and I'll tell you.'

In for a penny, in for a pound, I leaned in closer and kissed him on the lips. It wasn't a passionate one but he responded by pulling my head back to his and really giving me a kiss that was strong and cloying, his tongue pushing at my teeth which opened for his tongue to touch and play with mine. It was a real man-to-man type of kiss, taking it in turns to suck on each other's tongue in this kiss.

'We assume what is called the sixty-nine position. Upside down to each other. That's the way that the sucking of each other can be done at the same time,' he said, now turning himself round on the bed having his cock then just a few inches away from my face. The head was half out of the foreskin and of a purple colour from the blood that suffused it. I copied him as his hand took hold of mine in a firm grip.

His cock was hard and I could feel it pulsating in time with his heartbeat. The skin was soft and I found that it moved easily up and down over the solid flesh it covered. If I squeezed it on the upward moving of my hand, the eye would open and close as if it was winking at me.

I felt him take mine into his mouth that felt quite hot and I gave a gulp and was now about to find out if I would like doing what was now being done to me, and took the head of his cock into my mouth. It was just like a dog's rubber bone, only being a bit softer and as my lips had rolled down his foreskin, I then copied him in using my tongue to move over the bare flesh.

That's when my brain seemed to split in half and for both sides to start talking to each other in my mind, one speaking and the other answering.

What the fuck are you doing? Sucking his cock. What the fuck for? To try and give him the same pleasure he's giving me. His hand is moving up and down on your cock, you're not. Okay, move hand!

So I began to move that silken skin up and down, feeling it move so easily over the hard flesh that it covered. He's also using his saliva to make it easier in his mouth. Okay, I'll do the same, which I did. Is he enjoying it? He must be or he wouldn't be doing it. Are you enjoying it? To my surprise, yes. You know he swallows your cum? Yes. Will you swallow his? I don't know. We'll cross that bridge when the time comes. Don't you mean cums? Ha-ha, funny. You know you're not far from cumming? Yes, I can feel it.

I was now bucking my hips slightly upwards as I felt the surge coming up my cock and had it erupt into his mouth. His lips clamped tight round the base of the head as I pumped out all that I had generated inside my balls. Well he's now swallowing yours, the voice said, which was true for I felt that extra bit of suction as he did so.

Now comes the moment of truth. Another pun, the voice said as I felt him slightly stiffen and nearly gagged as the first salvo hit the roof of my mouth almost making me choke as it tried to slip down my throat. Then came more shots for his cum to join up again into one mass.

That's given you a thrill, hasn't it? Yes. Are you going to swallow it like he has yours? I.....

Then I gave a cough, the head still firmly in my mouth and I couldn't help but give a gulp and then had his cum slide down my throat.

Round the mouth, teeth and gums, look out stomach, here it comes, the voice chanted in my brain. But that was exactly what was happening. I had actually swallowed another man's cum after sucking his cock. My body was all of a tingle at having done this and I suddenly felt quite pleased with myself in doing so. If the truth be known, I really enjoyed sucking on him and was quite proud of myself for not having spat out his cum.

His hand was still squeezing its way up the shaft, him sucking out any residue left, so I did the same and even licked the head clean as he did in finishing of what is called a blow job. Blow job? It's more of a suck job with it being the exact opposite.

Peter had released my cock from his mouth and turned round on the bed and virtually threw himself on top of me to kiss me. It was an automatic move for my arms to move round his back to hold him as we kissed.

'You wonderful man,' he cried, breaking off his kissing of me. 'You actually swallowed it in your first time of sucking a cock.' His eyes were brighter than any sun as he looked down at me. 'Your cum is the best I've ever tasted, as well as you having the biggest cock too. I can't wait for it to be ready for you to fuck me again.'

Quid pro quo the voice asked? No fucking way was the answer.

With my bed being so narrow and with me lying on my back, he had to lay on his side as he began to stroke my body. He kept repeating at how lovely my cock was and that he couldn't wait for me to use it inside him. This was said in between the kisses he kept giving me on my cheek and neck. He even went as far as sucking and nibbling on one of my nipples as his hand moved up and down my chest and stomach, not missing out on my flaccid cock and balls.

It was nearly an hour before my cock was up to its full potential and had him give the head a suck before rolling a condom down on it and me moving to one side for him to get up onto his knees. We had shuffled around on the bed for him to assume the position on his hands and knees and for me to get in between his open legs and gave the cheeks of his bum a stroke before nestling the head of my covered cock to the entrance to his ass.

So on taking a deep breath, placed my hands on his hips and pushed myself forward. There was some resistance as the head of my cock fought the guardian of his ass, that being the sphincter muscle, that finally gave way for me to enter and delve deep into Peter's ass. He gave out another grunt and a whoosh of breath as I fully entered him, feeling his muscle flexing itself round the shaft that he so wanted to give him pleasure. Which I'm sure it did, for he began crooning as I moved myself back and forth in that tight orifice getting a similar pleasure in my fucking of him.

It wasn't long before I felt that my cum was agitated enough and had it shoot out and have him giving little squeals of delight, knowing that I was cumming inside him. Albeit being held back by the condom didn't stop him feeling the expansion of the head of my cock as I rendered up my emission of sperm.

'Wow!' he exclaimed. 'It feels even bigger than last time, Eddie.'

I could hear him panting and had his muscle moving faster than a fiddler's elbow round my cock. Not only was I drained of my cum but also felt exhausted in ramming my cock up his ass and now leaned over his rear end, panting, and trying to get more oxygen into my lungs.

'Nooo,' he cried out after I had straightened up and began to pull myself out of him, but I won the battle against that muscle of his and came out and sank back onto my heels. In spite of losing what he liked best, he was quick to turn round and pull the condom off of me and bend to lay down to take the head of my now steaming cock head into his mouth to suck out the residue as well as licking off the cum that still covered the head. He sucked me dry while cleaning the head with his tongue before coming up before me, to hold me tight as he kissed me.

As much as I had enjoyed sucking on his cock earlier, refrained from doing it again, well not this evening anyway, saving that for Sunday night. We finally broke apart and after both of us getting our breath back, I finally extricated myself from his arms and kisses and got off the bed and began to get dressed. He had a sulky expression on his face at me doing this, but didn't comment and got off the bed too and began to put his clothes on.

'You'll still let me come and sleep with you on Sunday night?' he asked.

'Of course, Peter. How else am I going to get to work early on Monday morning? I want to leave before seven to make the collections before heading off to Germany,' I told him.

He seemed somewhat mollified with me not saying that he could sleep over this night too, but it was my place here and I laid down the rules. So with another big hug and kisses, he finally said his goodbye and left me alone. Now if it had been Sam, I would have kept her there for the night. Instead, I went out and had dinner at the local Chinese restaurant before returning home and sleeping by myself.

SUNDAY, AS I predicted, Peter was at my door on the dot of nine that evening and so it was almost a repeat of what we did the day before, the difference being that he stayed the whole night and also had me fucking him early Monday morning. It had been a grand night of sex for both of us and I then realised that I was becoming bi-sexual in fucking him, being a male, and still wanting Sam to fuck too.

He was disgruntled again at me insisting that we couldn't fool around this morning as I wanted to have an early start, and so I had him drive me to the yard and already having the cash for fuel on the trip, soon drove out for my last run to Germany.

As on the other runs, everything went smoothly. Being on time to get my first load aboard the truck for Koln and then to the other factory for the load for Hamburg. Then down to Dover for my booking on the ferry. With those loads delivered and the collection from Amsterdam, the ferry back into England and the delivery of what I had collected, I was back in the yard late on the Saturday.

'You're late,' was the greeting by Sam as I got out of the cab and had her kiss me. I quickly broke this off as I saw Graham come out into the yard, damn sure he saw her kissing me.

'We were starting to get worried, Eddie,' he said as he approached.

'Sorry about that sir, but there was a hold up on the motorway. Three hours before the road was cleared of some accident ahead of me,' I told him.

'Well you're here now, safe and sound. Come and have dinner with us. I held it back until you returned,' he said, and noted that Sam had put her arm undermine and virtually dragged me over to the house. He also noticed her appropriation of me as the three of us went up to the house for dinner.

Sam even got me a drink in the lounge before dinner, ignoring her dad and letting him get his own. I apologised to the others of the family as I was sat down at the dining table, explaining that I didn't know that it was my fault that they had to wait. This was brushed aside by Graham and we had a good meal.

'With you being late by being held up, I've got the room ready for you to sleep over,' Sam said to me during the meal. I looked up alarmed at Graham, but saw that he had a smile on his face and gave me a nod. The bugger knew that it was her doing and that she would be sharing my bed for the night.

After that lovely meal cooked up by Sheila, I begged their forgiveness, but as a bed had been arranged for me, I wished to be excused, for I'd had a long day and was rather tired. This was accepted and I wished them all goodnight and went up to the room that I had occupied before. Within ten minutes of getting under the covers, I was fast asleep.

I don't know for how long I slept before being woken up with naked Sam getting into bed with me, but however long it was, it had rejuvenated me and I was able to see to her requirements. After much kissing between us and me having a massive erection, soon had myself inside her, giving her an orgasm at the same time as I had my cumming. With us both panting, I pulled out and rolled over onto my back but stopped Sam just as she was going to slide down the bed.

'Turn round Sam and let me see to you at the same time,' I said in a hoarse voice.

'Great,' she said and did as she was told and so with her getting astride of me, went down to suck on me and had her pussy down on my face for me to lick her at the same time. It didn't last long, what with me having already cummed, she soon turned round to lay on top of me for us to kiss, and it wasn't long before we fell asleep.

STEVE, THE usual driver for the Germany run, showed up for work, his leg now mended and fit for driving again. At the same time, two new trucks rolled into the yard. It was going to be four, but Graham had changed his mind as he had other plans that I found out later. So with two brand new trucks with Webb Haulage across the front and sides, having beneath the wording, a spider's web, the logo for the company, I had to tell Graham that they had arrived.

I went off to the house and was just approaching what was his office and study and the door hadn't been closed properly so I heard him talking to Sam. I stopped and didn't knock when I heard them talking about me.

'……..know you've had sex with him when he's stayed overnight. Do you love him?' Graham asked her.

'Daddy, I fell in love with him the first time I saw him in the yard. I had to find out what he was like in bed, and he's the man that I want to marry,' she told him and my heart glowed at hearing that.

'He must be good in bed then?' her father asked.

'The best daddy. Didn't you sleep with mom before you got married?' she asked.

'I'll admit that we did and never regretted it,' he said with a chuckle.

'You both must have loved it having four of us in the process. Why not more?' she asked.

'Four was enough we decided. If he asks you to marry him, how many will you want?' he asked in return.

'Four too, but maybe five, just to outdo you.'

They both laughed and I thought it was about time I made my presence known and knocked on the door.

'Enter,' Graham called out and I then went in.

'Hello, Sam. The two trucks have arrived, Graham,' I told him. These being the biggest that you can put out on the road.

'Great. Let's go and see them,' he said getting up from behind his desk. Both Sam and I followed him out of the house, having Sam stroking my bum as we went, though she dropped her hand when we entered the yard.

He walked round both trucks and seeing that they looked okay and had not been damaged before delivery, signed for them. He then got Peter to drive the two men who had driven the trucks to us, down to the station for them to return to their factory.

'What do you think of them, Eddie?' Graham asked after the two men had left with Peter.

'A nice addition to the fleet. I'll give them a check over, but I thought you wanted four?' I asked.

'I do, but there's an exhibition in a month's time and I want you and Peter to go and find me two like this that will suit us. You will have one and Steve will have the other, him having an H.G.V. licence and we'll employ another three later,' he said.

An H.G.V. is a Heavy Goods Vehicle for which you have to have a special licence to drive as opposed to our other trucks which could be driven by somebody with just a car licence. I was pleased at getting one and not being stuck in the yard all the time.

'You will be doing the local collections and deliveries while Steve can continue the European ones. I need you in the yard to keep up the good work in keeping the other vehicles on the road.'

So my job was really secure and that left the future which, after hearing him and Sam speaking, I now knew how to achieve. Now I always went in on a Saturday, only for the morning, doing odd chores and never asking for extra pay or overtime and so got lunch there instead. Before I left to go back to my digs, I asked Sam If she would like to have dinner with me that night. She agreed, and so came into town on time and met me at where I was living.

She came breezing in, straight into my arms for a kiss and I let her drag me into the bedroom. She quickly got her clothes off for me to see and admire her figure as she took off mine, revealing an erection that I obviously got at the thought of what we were about to do on the bed. She was quickly down onto her knees to take as much of my throbbing cock into her mouth to suck on me.

I could only take so much of that, so I pulled out and lifted her up to lay her on the bed. I climbed on top of both her and the bed and with her legs open ready for me, entered and fucked her. Now she was free to really give out quite a loud scream as she had her orgasm, something which she had to stifle when at her home. Her crying out like this made me cum, giving her all that I had while moving myself inside that lovely hot body of hers.

As per usual, after me pulling out, she went down and sucked on me till my cock was clean from both of our juices and after a bit more kissing of each other, the rumble in my stomach was heard and so we got up and dressed to go out for dinner.

I took her to the best restaurant in town and we had a lovely meal at our candlelit table. When we had finished our dessert and had coffee in front of us, I pulled out a small box, which I had bought that afternoon.

'Sam, will you marry me?' I asked, holding her hand across the table, nudging the box closer to her.

'Oh Eddie,' she said and started to cry. 'Yes. Yes, I will,' her hand now holding mine and giving it a squeeze.

'Why are you crying then?' I asked, a little bewildered.

'Because you've now made me so happy,' she replied, wiping her eyes with her fingers having let go of my hand. I now opened the box for her to see the engagement ring and heard her gasp. 'It's lovely,' she breathed, taking it out of the box. 'Put it on for me.'

I took the ring out of the box and with her left hand extended, slipped the ring on the correct finger, glad that I had managed to select the right size. With it firmly on her hand, she kept turning her hand one way and then the other to see the small diamonds sparkle in the candlelight.

'Kiss me Eddie,' she asked, and so I got up as she did too and went and kissed her, standing there in the middle of the restaurant, the couples at the nearest tables giving us strange looks. 'He's just asked me to marry him,' she said to them, showing them the ring and they all smiled with a couple giving her their congratulations.

We then moved over to where one of the waiters was seeing to the bills for each table and paid for our meal and we left and caught the bus to take us to her home. She held my hand the whole way, and kept looking at and admiring the ring on her finger. We held hands on leaving the bus to walk her home and as soon as we got inside, she almost screamed out to everyone that I had just proposed marriage to her and showed them all the ring.

There were smiles from all of them there and I had a beaming Graham shake my hand and then give Sam a kiss as others did the same. Michael then declared this was an occasion for a drink before and disappearing for a minute or two and coming back with three bottles of champagne as Sheila got out some glasses.

Graham had been astute with him laying these bottles in some time earlier and so we all had a glass after the cork was popped and our health was drunk. Sam couldn't stop blathering about how happy she now was and clung to me like a limpet as we drank all the champagne and we all got quite a bit tipsy as bottle after bottle was opened.

'Have you set a date yet?' Graham got around to asking.

'No,' said Sam. 'But the sooner the better.'

'You're not pregnant already?' he asked with a grin.

'No,' she grinned back at him, 'but I'll stop taking the pill as soon as we are married and I am then Mrs. Eddie May.'

I managed eventually to corner Peter away from the others.

'Peter,' I began. 'Will you be my best man?'

'By all means, Eddie,' he said. 'Thank you for asking.' Then giving me a sly look, 'Can I come on the honeymoon too?'

'Definitely not,' I replied.

'Er, with…with you then being my brother-in-law, will we still be able to….'

'Yes, but not at night for, er, well you know why,' I told him.

'Well I'd better make the most of our three nights at the exhibition then,' he grinned at me. That was because with the exhibition being over two days, he had booked us into a hotel for three nights. A room with a double bed I found out later, him driving us there the night before it opened and spending the last night there too before returning.

Sam broke up our talking by pulling me away from him and asking me when I wanted us to have the wedding so that arrangements could be made. We agreed to it being in two months' time.

'Now that we're engaged, I want you to move in here from where you are at present living,' she said.

'That's up to your father, not me,' I replied.

'I've already asked him and he has agreed to you having the spare bedroom, as long as I don't make too much noise at night,' she grinned at her not saying that he already knew that we slept together when I did sleep over. 'So you'll sleep here tonight and tomorrow you can move your things out of the hovel you've been staying in and bring them to what will be your new home.'

She seemed to have sorted this out already but it was me that would choose the place for our honeymoon, having an idea already as to where we should go for this and refused to tell her later when she asked me the question as to where this would be.

It wasn't long before we said goodnight to everyone and we went upstairs, her not caring now that they knew we would be sleeping together and came with me into the room that would be mine for two months after which it would be ours. It didn't take many minutes for us both to be naked and fall on the bed to kiss and fondle each other before me fucking my wife-to-be and had her sucking on me afterwards as I sucked at her pussy.

Though I hadn't had a lot to drink the night before, I was still as bleary eyed as the rest at breakfast, though mine was for lack of sleep having fucked Sam four times before falling asleep as dawn broke.

With Graham going to be the father of the bride, the onus was on him to see to the wedding breakfast with us having had set the date the night before, and I also learned that Graham had a mistress in town. He would spend every Tuesday night with her and with him having two holidays a year, took her with him. All the family knew of this and I got introduced to her later at the wedding reception, a widow who wanted her independence but still wanted sex too.

So I was now firmly ensconced in the family home and all the drivers got to hear of our engagement and got congratulations from them all and they had been told that they all were going to receive invitations to be at the wedding, though I think there was a bit of blackmail there in almost making it an order.

The time flew by and it came that Peter and I were to go off to the exhibition, us setting off after breakfast and arrived at the booked hotel in the mid-afternoon. He had stroked my thigh quite a few times on the journey saying that he had been looking forward to us being together in bed for three whole nights.

I wasn't surprised to find that the room booked had a big double bed and it wasn't long before we were on it, naked, to suck on each other's cocks, me now enjoying this form of male sex. Such was the need for both of us to release our cum and have our throbbing cocks deflate and so stop the pain they gave for being erect for so long. As it was close to dinner, we got dressed and went and had a decent meal and were soon in bed afterwards for me to fuck Peter but refused to let him fuck me, but would suck on him instead.

Before sleeping, I fucked him for the second time, loving to have my prick slide back and forth up in his tight ass and after stripping off the condom, he would suck out any residue of sperm while I sucked on him and got a mouthful of his semen to savour before swallowing. He still couldn't kiss me enough until we fell asleep.

WE WERE up fairly early so that we could have a decent shower, where we took turns washing the other, paying close attention to our cock and balls before getting dried and dressed and going down for breakfast. The exhibition opened at eight and it wasn't far from the hotel and after paying the entrance fee, wandered in to find a multitude of trucks of all types, many from Europe and Japan as well as English ones. Most were right hand drive though some were left. One of those we had in the yard was a left hand drive for use on the continent, making it much easier for the driver.

We walked all round that morning and then began again asking the sales person of those that caught our eye. Peter asking the mundane questions with me asking the technical ones. It was quite a long day for us seeing and asking our questions on only half of those that interested us, getting brochures as well as me filling quite a few pages of the pad I carried. At closing time, we went back to the hotel and had a couple of drinks before dinner, talking over those trucks that we had seen and the rest we should get round to the next day. Our entrance ticket was valid for both days. We had two bottles of wine with our dinner and I had two large Cointreau's afterwards with our coffee while he had Drambuie's.

We were half pissed by the time we got to our room, our clothes just being dropped on the floor as we staggered into bed to kiss and stroke each other. He got round to giving my cock a suck before fumbling with the condom and I had to help him in getting it on my cock properly before getting up behind him and pushing my now clad cock up into his ass. I suppose the advantage of being half drunk was that I was able to last longer in my fucking of him. Both of us getting the pleasure in doing so until I finally erupted and gave up my cum to the condom.

He managed to get the condom off of me after I had pulled out of his ass and had him give me another suck to clean up the head of my cock. When finished, he came up on his knees and pulled me to him for us to kiss, me getting a taste of my own cum from his lips.

'That was a lovely fuck, Eddie,' he slurred. 'Can I fuck you now? You'll enjoy it like I did.'

Now I'm blaming the booze we'd drunk for I went and said yes. His eyes lit up and he got another condom off the side table and got it out from its packet as I went down and gave the head of his erection a few brief sucks and helped him roll the condom down over the head of his cock and down the shaft. I turned round on my knees and he got behind me.

My body gave out a shiver when I felt the head of his clad cock touch the entrance to my ass, his hands then coming up onto my hips.

'Relax, Eddie. Stay relaxed and enjoy it,' he managed to say and I'm sure he was holding my hips to keep himself upright as he then leaned forward and I had his cock suddenly be pushed up inside me. It was that quick, my sphincter muscle didn't have time to react to his entry and so I then had his throbbing cock fully inside me with his thighs tight up to the cheeks of my bum.

Christ! You've gone and let him stick his cock up your ass, that voice in my head cried out. Too bloody late now, said the other one and this almost brought me sober at having agreed to let him fuck me. My muscle was now flexing itself around the shaft of his cock automatically, feeling it pulsating away, making all my insides tingle and the nerves sending little tremors throughout the whole of my body. Then he began to move and I felt him sliding it back and forth as he fucked me for the first time.

My heart was beating a tattoo inside my chest as he moved and the real problem was that I was beginning to enjoy feeling it smoothly moving inside me. So much so that I even began to dribble at the mouth at the pleasure I was getting at feeling his cock reaming my ass and wondered what it would be like if he wasn't wearing a condom. Would I be able to feel his cum when it shot out of the eye of his cock?

He kept on ploughing my virgin meadow for quite some minutes before he began pulling my hips back to his forward thrusts as they began getting faster, his thighs slamming themselves up against the cheeks of my bum, his balls also doing the same. He came to an almost stop as I felt the head of his cock expand a little more and knew that he was then cumming into the condom, getting his release and then had him come to a full stop, leaning over my rear end as he panted away.

'You lovely man,' he said and began to pull out. I was now making my muscle do its best to try and hold him there as I had really begun to enjoy him fucking me, and gave out a little cry when I felt it slip out. I don't know if it was instinctive or not, for I was quick to turn round and pull the condom off of his still hard and throbbing cock for me to take the head into my mouth to suck on it as I squeezed his hard cock, getting some of his cum to taste and swallow.

After a few minutes, he pulled my head up so that his cock slipped out of my mouth for me to straighten up to get a multitude of kisses from him as we both keeled over on the bed.

'I said it earlier and I'll say it again. You are a lovely man and I only wish that you could marry me instead of Sam, the lucky bitch,' he slurred. 'How was it? Did you enjoy it?'

'I….I can't really say as it was…indescribable,' I stammered.

'You'll let me fuck you again then?' he asked.

'I don't see why not, for I think I enjoyed it. What's it like without using a condom? Like having your cum in my mouth?' I asked.

'We call it bare back when a condom's not used, and yes, it's great to actually feel the cum hitting the insides. Next time we fuck, we'll go without using a rubber and you'll then feel the difference.'

We didn't do so that night for we were both soon asleep, cuddling each other.

WE BOTH had hangovers in the morning. Our shower helped somewhat, and we then went down for coffee, missing out on breakfast as neither of us wanted to eat right then. We bought a strip of Aspirins at the checking in desk and swallowed enough to clear our heads before returning to the exhibition. We had several cups of coffee there before we carried on our checking up on those trucks we were interested in but hadn't the time yesterday.

There was one item that really interested me, and that was an automatic jack for use when changing a wheel. Now all the large trailers that were fitted to the removable cab, all had double tyres, eight at the rear and four at the front. Now a truck would still roll with one of the two tyres being punctured but not for long when fully loaded and a man couldn't change that tyre on his own without special equipment. Well they had a jack there that worked like a compressor, being fitted to a connecting valve by the cab and it was the engine that gave it the power to lift the axle with the truck loaded with forty tons of goods. It also worked the tyre gun that enabled you to undo the nuts that held the wheel on and could also tighten them up when the wheel was replaced.

Now this was an item that I wanted each of the big trucks to carry with them and so got all the details about this to try and talk Graham into getting four of them. We also finally finished seeing all those that we wanted to see, me making lots of notes and Peter collecting the brochures and costs, etc.

'Let's not get drunk tonight,' Peter said. 'This will also be our last night that we can sleep together.' To which I agreed, and so we only had one beer at the bar and just one glass of wine with our dinner, after which, we went up to our room, undressed and got into bed. We both had erections that clashed as we kissed, Peter's hands moving up and down my body, building up a memory, I think.

'Fuck me first Eddie, and make it long and slow,' he breathed into my mouth.

'With or without a condom?' I asked, myself now stroking his body.

'Without, for I want to feel your cum as it hits the walls inside me,' he said, breaking away and going down and taking the head of my erection into his mouth to coat it with saliva as a lubricant. It was only in his hot mouth for a brief moment before he released me and got up onto his knees and waited for me to get up behind and in between his open legs. I nudged them further apart which made the cheeks of his bum stretch a little and I could clearly see the target and didn't have to hold my cock to be planted at the entrance to his ass. He gave out a shiver as he felt it touch him and holding his hips firmly, I pushed forward and saw the head of my cock move up into his ass. He gave out a grunt as I widened him and watched the head disappear and fully enter him until I was up inside that tight and all-encompassing canal.

He began to croon as I moved myself back and forth inside him, going slow, loving the pressure all round my cock, feeling his muscle constantly flexing itself round my cock and even began to croon too.

'Back in the saddle again, making love to my friend,' singing it softly and changing the words, 'him loving what I do, I love it too, fucking my friend once again.' He then began to softly sing a song.

'Row, row, row your boat, gently in the stream, merrily, merrily, merrily, your cock is such a dream.' As I was slowly moving myself back and forth, really enjoying this and hoped that I would feel the same when he was fucking me, for now having had him fuck me once, wanted him to do it again.

I then realised that I truly was bi-sexual, for I loved fucking Sam and now loved fucking Peter and wanted him to fuck me too.

Nature then took over and felt my seed boiling up, wanting release from my balls. I gripped his hips tighter, pulling his ass back onto me as I rammed forward and began to give him my cum. He gave out little squeals of delight as he felt me beginning to coat the insides of his channel as I unloaded the cum from my balls. I was grunting at every shot until I was empty and leaned over his rear, breathing heavily, making my cock twitch inside him, running my fingernails up and down the sides of his chest, making his body give out shivers.

'Fucking awesome Eddie. Feeling your cum hitting the insides of me,' he panted. 'You're going to love it too.'

I gave out a grunt and pulled out of him to little cries from him as his muscle was clenched tight round my cock, trying to grip and hold me there as it left his body. There was no point in sitting back on my heels for he wasn't going to suck on my cock now, and so I got off the bed, staggering slightly as I went off to the bathroom to wash my cock at the basin there.

I looked up into the mirror there and saw the sick grin on my face knowing that in a couple of minutes, I was going to have his cock up my ass for the second time. Let's just hope that I will enjoy it as much as he does, I said to myself. I finished washing myself carefully and after drying my cock and balls, for they had got wet too, went back into the bedroom to see Peter lying on the bed with a big grin on his face and his erect cock lying up on his stomach.

'Come and kiss me lover,' he said in a low and melodious voice as he opened his arms. I gave him back a smile, trying not to have the same expression on my face that I had seen in the mirror. I got on as his arms came round me and we kissed, his cock now touching my stomach as he half rolled towards me.

'I hope you will love us fucking as I did,' he said after our kisses and moved away and held his cock upright. 'Give it a few sucks and cover it with your saliva.'

This I did, now loving to have this throbbing cock head in my mouth and worked my saliva all over the head before releasing him and rolling over onto my front before getting up onto my knees as he moved down the bed.

'The secret is to relax,' he said as he nudged my legs further apart as I had done to him. His hands came onto my hips and I gave out a shiver as I felt the head of his cock touch my asshole. 'Relax and enjoy it,' he said again and I felt the pressure as he leaned forward with his cock trying to gain entrance to my ass.

As much as my mind was willing my body to relax, the muscle there just wouldn't obey the command from my mind, and kept trying to stop the entry. I was beginning to get some pain as it was being stretched and gave out a jerk as his hand suddenly gave a cheek of my bum a hefty smack.

It was a shock, but it worked for the head of his cock was then inside me and quickly followed by the shaft as his thighs came up to my bum, throbbing away inside me. The pain slight now that his cock was fully inside me, feeling it pulsating away as his hands now firmly held me as he began to slowly pull back and then move forward. Now I was beginning to enjoy it moving inside me and suddenly gave out a gasp and realised that I had been holding my breath and now took in big gulps of air. I'm sure that my face had been a bright red from holding my breath that long.

But now I was enjoying the slow moving of his cock inside me, flexing my muscle round the shaft, getting tingles up and down my spine at each twitch he gave it as it moved in and out. I was really loving having it where it was and hoped he could last for more than a few minutes. But like me, he could only hold back from cumming for only a short time and I felt him start to move a little faster, ramming his thighs up to me as his hands pulled me back onto his throbbing cock.

I felt the head start to expand a little and then suddenly felt his first salvo of cum hit the walls of my channel. I gave out a thrilling gasp at feeling his cum begin to spray my insides. It was, as he said, awesome, having the insides of my ass coated with his cum. I was now hooked on bare back sex, really feeling his cock move inside me and feeling his cum shoot out of the eye.

I gave out a cry as I felt him pulling out and tried to hold it inside me and had some pain as the head expanded me again, though not as bad as an entry for the muscle didn't try to really stop anything when leaving your ass. The air felt cold round my shrinking hole as I felt the bed sag as he got off to go and wash himself and I rolled onto my side, feeling the glow that was inside me and now wanted him to fuck me again when he was up and ready.

Like him, I waited with open arms for him to come back onto the bed for me to kiss him for the pleasure he had given me, knowing that he'd had the same in his fucking of me. We kissed and stroked each other for nearly an hour until our cocks were once again rampant and went into the sixty-nine position to suck, chew and lick each other's cock until we had them erupt the cum for us to savour and swallow.

It was another hour before we fucked each other again, getting the same thrill as before, having us feel the cum being sprayed inside our ass and with it being well after midnight after we'd washed ourselves, it wasn't long before we went to sleep in each other's arms.

IT WAS not a fuck we had after waking up, but a mutual sucking of each other before having our shower and getting dressed, vacating the bedroom and taking our bags downstairs to leave with the concierge while we had our breakfast. After paying the bill, we took our bags down to the hotel's garage and put them in the car and got in for Peter to then drive us back home.

I was already calling where I had now moved into as home, for there, was my future wife that would be waiting for me to fuck her, though not being fucked in return like my future brother-in-law had. We didn't rush and we arrived back at the yard just in time for dinner, being rather hungry as we didn't stop for lunch on the way back.

Sam literally threw herself into my arms as I got out of the car, kissing me like mad as Peter got our bags out and finally being able to extract myself from Sam's exuberant greeting, followed him into the house. Graham greeted us with Michael being there too, and we went into the study and had a drink as Peter and I told him of the exhibition. This carried on during dinner and we carried on afterwards, with both of the others looking at the brochures that Peter had brought with us and me also reading out the notes that I had made.

Graham was impressed with the jack that I told him about and agreed to buying one at least to see for himself how good it was. We talked about what we had seen at the exhibition for over an hour and it wasn't until Peter yawned did we realise that it was close on midnight. So Graham called it a night and told us to go to bed. Peter looked at me wondering if his father knew that he was gay and was alluding that us two went to bed together. I shook my head as though trying to stay awake, and Peter got the message and we said our goodnights to Graham and went upstairs to bed. Peter into his room and me into mine.

It was a good job that we parted out in the hall for I found Sam already in my bed.

'About time you came to bed,' she said in a sullen voice.

'Blame your father for me not coming up earlier, for I wanted to very much. Also to clear the air, you don't tell me when and what time I should be in bed. That is my decision, not yours, do you understand?' I said, a little on the harsh side, but she had better learn now before we got married that I was my own man and no woman was going to rule me.

'I'm sorry, Eddie. I didn't mean to sound like a shrew,' she said contritely.

'Okay. I wanted to come to bed much earlier, but it was business that held me back for he is the boss,' I said as I began to get undressed.

As I was doing that, she pulled the nightgown she had been wearing over her head, for me to see her lovely tits out in view for me, which gave my cock that extra bit of strength to come up into a fucking mode. If the truth be known, I would rather have gone straight to sleep, but she was waiting there and I couldn't refuse what she wanted from me.

I got into bed and into her arms where we kissed as I moulded a tit in my hand and her hand drifted down the bed to rub my erection.

'I've missed having this, Eddie. I've been waiting all day for you to come home and fuck me. You will, won't you?' she asked, a pleading look on her face.

'Of course darling,' I said, rolling her onto her back and moving over on top of her to kiss my way down to kiss and nibble at a nipple before getting up onto my elbows and letting her feel my throbbing cock move between her legs and probe the entrance to her pussy.

'Oh Eddie,' she groaned as her legs widened and began to lift up in the air as my cock slid smoothly inside the heat of her oven and began to fuck my future wife. As tired as I was, I managed to keep ploughing her meadow until she began bucking beneath me in the throes of having her orgasm, me then letting go of my cum and had it spray her insides. An arm had left my shoulder and she used her hand to stifle the scream that she would have given at having her orgasm. Her eyes shining as she slumped back down on the bed and pulled me down to squash her tits as she showered my face with kisses.

Having now fucked her, I was really knackered and it seemed a great effort to pull myself out of her and thankfully rolled off of her onto my back and closed my eyes as she went down to suck any cum from the head of my dick. I managed to stay awake until she'd finished sucking on me and came back up the bed to kiss me.

'Sorry darling, but I'm dog tired and can hardly keep my eyes open,' I mumbled, giving her one last kiss before leaning back on the pillow and falling asleep.

I CAME awake to find I was alone in my bed, and looked at the bedside cock.

'Shit!' I exclaimed, for it was showing that it was just on ten o'clock. I scrambled out of bed and had a quick shit, shave, shower and shampoo. The four S's before getting dressed and going downstairs to find Sam and Katie in the kitchen.

'You should have come and woke me up,' I said to Sam, wording it like that because of Katie being there. 'I'm late for work.'

'Sit down and have some breakfast,' she said. 'Dad said you and Peter could have the morning off, and he's not even up yet.' So I left the kitchen mumbling and went and sat down at the dining table and a few minutes later, had breakfast put in front of me. I was halfway through when Peter came in, looking worse that I felt.

'You're having a late breakfast,' he said.

'I overslept,' I managed to say with a mouthful of food.

'So did I. Any left?' he asked.

'The girls are in the kitchen. Go and ask them,' I told him. He went off and was back a minute later to sit down, shortly to be followed with his breakfast. I stayed there having a second cup of coffee to his one before we both left the dining room and went out into the yard. Steve's big truck was still there but he wasn't. I went into the office where Michael worked.

'Where's Steve?' I asked.

'Brian phoned in sick and so he's taken his truck out,' was the answer from Michael.

'What did you think about the jack I talked about last night?' I asked him.

'Sounds great. I was on the phone to them this morning and sent Roger off to pick one up, so we'll see it later today,' he replied.

'That's good. I'd better get out there and fix up a bracket for it on the truck. I've already got the measurements for it,' I told him and went out and got the welding kit and some metal steel strips that I could bend and make the cradle to hold it. I also made the means of connecting it to be worked from the truck's engine and had it all ready by mid-afternoon just before Roger drove into the yard having made his deliveries and had collected the jack.

With it unloaded, Graham came out as well as Michael and Peter for me to show them how it worked and it did exactly what it said on the side. It even fitted nicely into the frame that I had made and could also be locked up with the key to the massive lock, added to the truck's ignition and door keys. I later showed Steve how it worked so that he knew he would be able to change a tyre if he had to. It was four months before he had to use it and was pleased with being able to do so and not lose time in having to wait for some garage hands coming out to find him and do the job that he was now able to do himself.

TIME WAS flying by and it was soon only a week away from me marrying Sam. She'd already had her wedding dress made and I had a new suit, well the only one, and Graham had made all the arrangements, that being the actual wedding and the reception. I too had already booked our honeymoon, but wouldn't tell anyone where we would be going. I'd also remembered to buy a wedding ring, well two really. One for Sam and one for myself.

We were still sleeping and having sex together every night and I had the odd fling with Peter when Sam wasn't around. Then before I knew it, my wedding day came round. Michael and Sheila had taken it upon themselves to do the organisation of things. Michael seeing to the means of transport, well it was his line of work anyway, while Sheila saw to the catering side, her forte.

Sam didn't sleep with me the night before as she had been told that we shouldn't see each other on that day until we were in the church.

So I had Peter in my room that night, not the whole night, but just long enough for us both to fuck each other as well as sucking on our respective cocks.

Two Bentley chauffeured cars turned up in the yard as did a minibus. The two cars were for Sam and Graham to be in one, Michael, Sheila, Katie and Peter to be in the other. The minibus was for me and all the drivers to be taken to the church before the cars.

Peter had seen that I was properly shaven and helped me dress, sucking on my cock in the process, taking my cum to calm me down for I was a bag of nerves. Seeing to my tie and my button hole flower before saying that I was then fit to be in the church to get married. I passed over the rings that he was to give us during the ceremony and with him already dressed, escorted me down and out into the yard where the firm's drivers were waiting, all dressed up in their Sunday best and were given button hole flowers handed out by Peter. He would be staying to come with the others before Sam and Graham and would meet me in the church.

The minibus took off and I got quite a bit of ribbing from the drivers on the way there, some annoyed at me taking Sam out of circulation which showed that they would have liked the chance to marry her. We duly arrived and went inside the church and saw that Graham hadn't stinted over the arrangements. There were flowers beyond count along the side walls as well as in the Chancery, and a choir consisting of at least twelve young boys.

The vicar greeted me and we shook hands and it was just a matter of then waiting for the arrival of Peter and the following arrival of Graham and Sam. The drivers had stayed outside to see Sam's arrival and would come in before she did. Even so, there were quite a few people already inside, leaving the two front rows of the pews empty. I wasn't long standing alone in front of the vicar before Peter came and stood beside me, the others that had been in the car following him and taking their places in the front pews, shortly to be followed by the drivers to take their places. This told me that Sam and Graham had arrived.

The organist had been softly playing some ancient hymns until he was given the signal that the bride to be was entering the church when he then crashed out the wedding march. I hadn't had any breakfast and my stomach was churning itself over and over with the butterflies that were driving me mad inside. With the organ now playing the march, I couldn't stop myself from looking back and my heart leapt into my mouth at seeing Sam dressed in her wedding gown and looking so radiant and beautiful, coming down the aisle with her arm in that of her flushed looking father.

I turned back to face the vicar as they got closer and then felt her arm brush mine as she came and stood on my left, Graham on the other side to her left as I had Peter on my right. The wedding march came to a close and fell silent as the vicar, standing one step up higher than us before him, opened his book and began the service.

'Dearly beloved. We are gathered here today......... '

Well you know all what he says so there's no need for me to repeat it. He asked the questions that we both answered and Peter passed me the ring to put on her finger and a few words later, he spoke the usual words.

'......I now pronounce you man and wife. You may kiss the bride.'

Sam turned to me lifting her veil, her eyes positively glowing, her cheeks on the red side as our heads moved towards each other. We kissed to then have all those inside the church start to clap their hands and cheer at being at this, to me, grand event.

The organist started playing again and me and my wife, Sam, followed the vicar into the vestry to sign the book. We were applauded again as I walked my bride down the aisle to step outside to have many photographs taken. Us alone, then with Graham, another with Michael, Sheila, Katie and Peter. Another with the vicar. Then others from the firm and more of others too. Then of Sam and I entering the car that had brought her to the church, more taken of us inside and as we drove off to the hotel where the reception was being held.

Here more were taken. Us sitting in the middle of the top table, cutting the fourtiered wedding cake. Us passing out slices to those who were there which must have been at least sixty persons, most of whom I had no knowledge of. I believe and had others say so later, that the whole thing had been a great success. The service in the church, the reception, everything went off very well and couldn't be faulted. But like everything else, it had to come to an end and Sam and I were the first to leave, letting those who wished to stay, to finish off the champagne and other drinks as we got into the car and were driven off home.

We thanked the driver when we arrived and I passed him a ten pound note as a tip before escorting my new wife and lover up to what would now officially be our room. Sam took off her veil and the tiara that held it in place before we went into each other's arms to kiss.

'Well Sam, how do you like now being called Mrs. May instead of Miss Webb?' I asked.

'I love it as I love the man I just married. Shall we consummate the marriage then?' she asked with a sly smile.

'Yes, but in a different way,' I said. 'Keep the dress on,' I said as I opened my trousers and took them off, letting her see that I already had an erection, her eyes having a query in them as I pulled a chair up to us and I sat down on it, my cock sticking up from my groin. 'Now lift up the dress and sit on this.' The penny then dropped and she gave me a grin and hoisted up the front of her dress, letting me see that she wasn't wearing any panties. She got astride of my legs and lowered herself down to have my cock then move up into her wet pussy until she was sitting on my thighs with my throbbing cock stuck up inside her.

I pulled her forward and kissed her as I began to bounce her up and down on my cock, her then helping by lifting herself at the same time and so we fucked in that position until I gave her my cum as she had her orgasm. We had been kissing each other in our throes of making love in this fashion and held each other tight as we had our release. After a few minutes, she got up off of me and moving the front of her dress to the side, went down onto her knees and began to suck my still hard and wet cock for another few minutes before letting go of it and getting up, asking me to help her off with her dress, which I did for her then to put it on a hanger and away into her wardrobe.

'I'm saving that for when my daughter gets married,' she told me.

'Only one?' I asked with a smile.

'Of course not, darling. Five at least,' she said as she took off what little she had left on that lovely body that was now all mine.

'Five girls?' I cried.

'Well I hope three of the five are boys,' she said as she began to take my shirt off.

'Why five?' I asked, taking my own socks off.

'Well daddy had four children. I want to go one better than him and mother. Do you think we could work it so that they are all born in the month of May?'

I had to laugh at that. 'Maybe,' I said, picking her up and carrying her to the bed and throwing her on it first before climbing on to go into her arms for us to kiss and stroke each other.

'When are we going on our honeymoon?' she asked, really knowing damn well when.

'The day after tomorrow,' I replied.

'Where?' she asked coyly.

'You'll find out at the airport,' I said and got a slap.

'Now you're being cruel,' she pouted.

'If I was cruel, it would be me going on my own,' I said, for which I got another slap, but then I grabbed her and pulled her over across my thighs and began to smack her bottom.

'You beast!' she cried.

'Yes. I'm the beast and you're the beauty,' I replied and found that I was getting another hard on by having her spread over my lap as I smacked her backside. 'And this beast is going to fuck his beauty.'

I pushed her over onto her back and quickly got between her legs that had opened, a big smile on her face as I sunk my cock deep into her pussy and once again, brought her up to another orgasm, with me sadly, not having any cum left inside my balls to give her, hard as I was.

'Twice inside of fifteen minutes,' she gasped. 'You should smack me more often.'

'If you enjoyed it, then I won't,' I said.

'Sadist!'

'Masochist!'

'Beast!'

'Beauty!' and she then laughed and hugged me as we kissed.

We lay there for at least an hour saying sweet things to each other in between kisses until I was up hard again with her then wanting me to fuck her with what she could feel against her thigh. I obliged and got on top of her and entered her once again. I was slowly moving myself in that lovely heated interior when she asked the questioned that I had hoped that she wouldn't.

'When you were in the hotel with Peter for three nights, did you have sex with him?' was the question.

'Well he wanted it, so yes, I did,' I told her.

'Did you fuck him?'

'Yes. And I used a condom before you ask,' I replied.

'Did…did he fuck you?' was the question I dreaded, but she then forestalled me. 'No! Don't tell me. I don't want to know,' she pleaded. So I didn't tell her, thank fuck for that. She was silent for a few moments as I still kept moving myself slowly inside her. 'What was it like?'

'Tighter than you and not so good, but it was what he wanted. He seems to enjoy it. Why do you ask? Is it that you want, to see me fucking him?'

'No. That's not what I was thinking of. It's …it's just that I don't want to lose you to him,' she said in a low voice, tears forming in her eyes.

'Sam darling, you are one I love. I love what we are doing now, giving us both pleasure and cumming at the same time. Two men can't do that,' I said, now beginning to move myself faster inside her hot pussy, making her concentrate on having her orgasm which wasn't long in coming (pun?). She began to buck beneath me and as she screamed out in the throes of this, I let go and gave her my cum at the same time.

We didn't go downstairs for dinner, but fucked ourselves silly that night.

WE HAD sex again on waking up in the morning and even had a shower together, each washing the other and having kisses in between, before getting out and drying ourselves before getting dressed and going downstairs for breakfast.

'Two more for breakfast, Sheila,' Graham called out to the kitchen. 'The lovebirds have arrived,' he chuckled. 'Sleep well?' He laughed out loud. 'I thought you were murdering her with the screams she gave out.'

'Pay no attention to him, Eddie. He's just jealous with him only getting his end away once a week,' Sam said, making Graham splutter.

'What do you mean by that, girl?' he asked.

'Oh come off it, dad. We all know you've got a mistress in town. And the fact that you take her away with you on your twice yearly holiday,' Sam retorted, and he had the grace to blush and then give her a grin.

'How long have you known?' he asked.

'For bloody years. Why haven't you married her?' she asked.

'She wants to keep her independence,' was the soft reply. The subject was dropped when Sheila brought in our breakfast, a big smile of her face.

'Eat it all, for you need to keep your strength up,' she chuckled as she gave me my plate. 'Isn't marriage wonderful?' she said, first looking at Sam and then at Michael, making him blush.

'It shore is,' Sam drawled. Mangling her Americanism.

'When are you leaving for the honeymoon?' Graham asked me.

'We leave early tomorrow morning,' I replied. 'The flight is at eight o'clock.'

'I wish I was going,' said Peter, a downcast expression on his face, and his comment was ignored.

'Where will it be?' Graham asked slyly, knowing that I had refused to tell him earlier.

'I'll let you know just before we leave,' I grinned back at him.

That was it at breakfast and though I was officially on holiday and not having to work, still checked out what trucks were still in the yard and seeing that Sam had everything packed as we would be leaving the house at four in the morning to be at the airport in time for the flight.

We only had sex once that night, what with us having to get up at three in the morning, a taxi being ordered for four a.m. to take us directly to the airport. The alarm woke us and still being bleary eyed, had our shower and got dressed and went downstairs and was surprised to see Graham up and helped us with the two cases when the taxi pulled up outside.

'Are you going to tell me where you're going?' he asked me.

I whispered the answer in his ear. 'The Bahamas, and we'll send you a card on arrival.'

'Lucky devil,' he chuckled. 'Now both of you have a good honeymoon and don't get sunburnt,' and chuckled when I scowled at him as I got into the taxi. He waved at us as we drove out of the yard, both Sam and I waving back at him and settled down for the long ride to the airport. I even had Sam fall asleep on the journey.

We arrived at the airport on time and joined the small queue at the check in desk.

'Lyon's Airways?' Sam said, looking at the sign above and behind the desk. 'Never heard of them.'

'It's developed over the years,' I told her. 'It has only the one destination from this airport.'

'And where's that?' she asked as our suitcases were weighed.

'You'll find out shortly,' I told her as I took our boarding cards and we went off through passport control, not having any trouble there and on to the waiting lounge until our flight was called.

'How shortly?' she asked as we sat down and taking hold of my hand.

'When we get aboard the plane,' I said.

'I've never been in a plane before,' she said and I felt her trembling..

'You'll enjoy it, believe me. And when on board, you'll find out where we are going,' I told her. 'I was thinking…..'

'That's dangerous,' she interrupted.

'….about what you said in having a child…….'

'Children,' she interrupted me again.

'Children, to be born in May…..'

'I'm glad that it is May now. The month we got married and I want all the children to be born in May,' she wistfully.

'Will you stop interrupting me,' I said.

'Sorry. You were saying?'

'Pregnancy takes roughly nine months and nine days, give or take a week. So to have a child, stop!' I said, putting my hand to her mouth. 'Children. That means you need to conceive in August. So stay on the pill until near the end of July,' finally having got out what I was saying.

'It will be nice to have all the May's born in May. I wish I had been born in May,' she said with a sigh. 'When were you born?'

'August the 5th,' I told her.

'The same day as me,' she cried. 'That's an omen! So we can celebrate our birthdays together and start to produce our children then. How wonderful.'

That was all we could say then for the tannoy asked us in the lounge that we could now board our plane. There was about twenty of us there, and we all followed the stewardess, who was dressed in a smart light blue uniform, through the exit and down a ramp and out onto the tarmac.

'That's a small plane,' Sam said as we were led across the tarmac towards it. The logo telling everyone that it was Lyon Airways in big letters down the side.

'It's big enough to take us where we are going,' I told her.

'Where's that?' she asked.

'Shut up,' I almost snarled and got a grin from her.

We followed some of the other passengers up the short steps and entered the small aircraft and I noticed that it only had twenty seats and that they all had plenty of leg room, and all in pairs so there was only five sets either side. I led Sam up to the last pair at the end and pushed her to sit next to the window.

The light above us said to fix our seat belts, me having to help Sam do this with it being her first time and by the time that was done, the plane gave a short jerk and began to slowly move off to follow the side road that led to the takeoff end of the runway. The tannoy crackled.

'This is the captain speaking. We'll be taking off in the next minute or two, so please make sure that your seat belt is safely secured. We will be flying at sixteen thousand feet at a speed of four hundred and fifty miles an hour and expect to land at Nassau at eleven a.m. local time. Breakfast will be served shortly. Relax and enjoy the flight,' and the tannoy clicked off. The stewardess had checked that all were belted up before sitting on a folding seat near the front.

'Where's Nassau?' Sam whispered to me.

'Didn't you do geography at school? It's the capitol of the Bahamas, in the Caribbean,' I told her.

'Oooh, I've heard of that, but never been there,' she said and then gripped my arm as the plane gave a forward leap and shot off down the runaway. It, being a small plane and quite light, didn't have to go far before lifting up at a steep angle, making Sam give out a gasp as seeing the ground suddenly disappearing from view. The plane passed through some wispy clouds and emerged into bright sunlight.

'Oh look,' Sam cried. 'Look at the clouds down there. Just like a white blanket.' I had to grin at her exuberance and released our belts as the stewardess came along the short aisle with a drinks trolley. Those in front were served first and when she got to us, she asked with a smile.

'I believe that you are the honeymoon couple,' and Sam gushed that we were. 'Well compliments of Lyons Airways, it is champagne for you,' and placed two glasses on the trays that I had pulled down that had been fixed to the seat in front as she popped the cork and poured us out some champagne and then placed the bottle on my tray. 'Congratulations.

Breakfast will be along in a minute or two,' and gave us a choice of what to eat. We both picked the same.

Sam lifted her glass up, 'Cheers,' she said as I lifted mine and we clinked them together before taking a few sips. 'Will we have to pay for this?' she asked.

'No. It's complementary, free. The whole of the holiday is inclusive, so you eat and drink as much as you want on the island,' I told her.

'Island?' she queried.

'Yes. It's an island resort. We'll land at Nassau on this plane and then have a small sea plane take us to the island where we can then enjoy ourselves.' We stopped speaking then as breakfast came along and it was by far much better than the K rations that I used to have when flying with the army.

With this eaten and our empty trays taken away, I said to Sam, 'Are you tired?'

'No. I'm too excited with this,' she exclaimed.

'Well I am and want to go to bed,' I said, getting up from my seat.

'Bed? On a plane?' she asked wide eyed. I grinned at her and took her hand to help her up as the stewardess came up to us.

'It's the first door on the left,' she said to me with a smile. I then walked that short distance and opened the door and ushered Sam inside.

'A fucking bed!' she exclaimed and I laughed.

'That's exactly what it is,' and pulled her to me and kissed her, 'and we are going to join the Mile High Club.'

'What's that?' she asked.

'That's for people who have sex while over a mile high in the sky as we are now,' I told her as I began to take her clothes off until she was naked and she got onto the bed and looked out of the window at the clouds far beneath us as I took my clothes off and got on the bed alongside her.

'Can I look out of the window while we're doing it?' she asked with a grin.

'Certainly,' I said, holding my cock up erect. She smiled at me and bent round and took the head into her hot mouth and gave me a few sucks and a lick before moving across me and straddling my thighs and slowly lowered her body down until the head of my cock was inside her pussy before letting go of it for her to sink down until she was sitting on my thighs with my throbbing cock fully inside her.

'Oh this is grand. A flying fuck on a flying fucking mattress,' she exclaimed, starting to bounce up and down on me. Her tits were bouncing about too and so I reached up and began to squeeze them with my hands as she technically fucked herself on top of me. 'This is fucking wonderful,' she gasped and brought her hands up to cover mine and pressed them harder to her chest as she began to have her orgasm. She gave out a muted scream when this happened and I then let go and had my cum shoot up inside her to then collide with her juices on the way down.

She finally collapsed on top of me, panting away, to kiss me in between taking deep breaths. 'You wonderful man, giving me this pleasure of having a fuck on a plane high up in the sky.'

'The pleasure's mine too with you being pleased as well as now being my wife for us to do this,' I said, really as happy as she was. She soon rose up for my cock to slide out of her where she then went down and sucked on it for a couple of minutes before moving back up to give me a wet kiss.

With us cuddling each other, we fell asleep. I was woken up by the bedside phone ringing to find it was the stewardess.

'Lunch will be served in half an hour and we'll be landing half an hour after that,' she said.

'Thank you. We'll be out by then,' I said, putting the phone down and rolling over to Sam who had also woken up. 'We've got half an hour. My turn to join the Mile High Club,' I said as I moved over on her and gave her my erection and I was then able to see the lower clouds as I ploughed my way in and out of her wet pussy until she had another orgasm and me cumming inside her at the same time.

This flying bedroom also had a small, very small, shower room with a wash basin and toilet, though only big enough for one person at a time, but a means to ablute (ablutions) and have a shower. This was done inside that half hour and were soon back in our seats for lunch and shortly after that, we landed in Nassau. Sam got a thrill at watching us cross the harbour to turn round and land on the airport's runway.

We all disembarked, the stewardess thanking everyone for flying Lyons Airway and wished us luck as we passed and thanked her for the lovely treatment on the flight. All the baggage was quickly off and the others had some cars waiting to take them to the waiting lounge down by the harbour while we were escorted to a small seaplane where our bags were put aboard as our passports were quickly glanced at before we climbed aboard, being the only two to be flown out to the island first. The other passengers, when at the hotel's lounge, could either go by boat to the island or wait for the seaplane to return to land in the harbour, though it could only carry four at a time.

But we were quickly in the air and in less than ten minutes flew across and round the small island below before landing on the sea and gently coasted up to the jetty. One of the hotel staff took hold of the plane's tie up rope to secure it to the jetty. Another took our two bags out of the plane and the other helped Sam out of the plane onto the jetty and left me to get out myself. Our bags were taken away and we were escorted up to the reception desk as the plane was released to fly back to Nassau to collect more guests.

'Welcome Mr. May and of course, the new Mrs. May,' the guy behind the counter said.

'Were there other Mrs. May's then?' Sam asked.

'Sorry ma'am, I worded that wrong. You are the only Mrs. May that has arrived on the island and we welcome you, this being your honeymoon, and we hope that your stay here will be remembered for years to come,' he replied at his faux pas. 'You have the bridal suite, house number one. Please sign in sir,' he said to me, which I did and was then escorted to what would be our dwelling for the next two weeks.

We skirted the pool and went down a path through the palm trees to what would be our abode for the duration. The building itself was two storied, the lower ones being those with double beds and the upper ones having single beds. Ours of course had a double bed and we found that it was bigger than most hotels and the bathroom was a delight, having learned that you would have the room to be able to swing a cat round in it. This had been built by the young woman who had bought and designed the island at the tender age of being in her young twenties, back in the fifties. (Ed: Read 'Francis' in these editions as to how this island came to be.)

The guy that had escorted us to our suite told us that lunch would soon be served and I thanked him, though we weren't hungry for food as we had eaten on the plane. We were hungry for sex.

As soon as he had left, our clothes were off and we had a lovely session of making love in the only way we knew how. Between our arrival and time for dinner, we fucked twice with her going down on me afterwards and me once going down and sucking at her pussy.

We redressed to go up to the bar for a drink before dinner, all paid for in the overall cost before we had one of the best meals I had ever tasted. I might add now, that every meal we had on the island couldn't be faulted. Lobster, Crab, Prawns and any other fish that could be caught by Nassau's local fishermen. The same applied to the variety of meats available too.

After such a wonderful dinner, we had a couple of drinks at the bar before returning to our suite and spent the rest of the night having beautiful sex between us. Having had many good hours of sleep on the plane, we were able to last much longer than normal in our fucking and sucking between us. But the best was yet to come.

AFTER HAVING coffee delivered to our room in the morning, I again mounted Sam, and gave her all of my night's accumulation of sperm, bringing her up to an orgasm and had her again, suck on my wet cock after having pulled out of her.

We showered and dressed to go and have breakfast and ordered a hamper for us to take off to the secluded beach where clothing was optional. Sam didn't twig onto this until we were on a deserted beach, being the first ones there when I told her that this beach was off limits to staff and solely for the guests that required privacy to be able to sunbathe without clothing being worn.

'A nudist beach?' Sam exclaimed.

'Yes,' I grinned, stripping of the shorts that I was wearing and spread out the towels from our room and laid down, my erect cock now lying up on my stomach.

'What will people say if they saw you like this?' she cried out in alarm.

'Well the women would say that you were damn lucky to have a man like me with you, and wish they could change places,' I said with a grin.

'You expect me to strip off and be naked for other men to ogle me?' she cried.

'Darling, you'll be the envy of all the other women who come here and be lusted for by all the men, so don't be such a prude and get off what little you have on and let's get a tan all over our bodies,' I told her.

She slowly succumbed and took off what she was wearing to be as naked as the day she was born and after a few days, became blasé about revealing the lovely figure she had as she got many admiring glances from other men that used this private nudist beach. But after seeing what they had to display, said that I came out tops in the rampant cock stakes. I returned the compliment by saying that she had a far better figure than the harridans that we saw.

So we would spend most days on that nudist beach, getting our bodies really tanned, both front and back, though she insisted that when I was lying on my back, at least covered my cock so as not to get it sunburnt and be of no use to her when we went to bed.

Another highlight was to take her down to the water's edge for an evening and with the surf washing against our bodies, fuck her as what wasn't shown in that film 'From Here to Eternity'. She said that she got a thrill when we did so, with me up hard inside her as we fucked and her also feeling the cool water washing around her back and feeling the sand move under her as the water receded. To her, it was most erotic.

We never got to use the swimming pool just outside of the lounge, spending nearly every day out on this beach. Not only getting a lovely tan on our bodies but also having sex out there on the open. Though for the first week, she wouldn't, but after seeing other couples having sex, didn't mind us doing the same. One of the highlights in doing this down on that beach, was to see two men having sex as we did.

They were only a few feet away from us on my side as we lay on the beach towels. They had seen me fucking Sam and so decided that is was alright if they did the same. I had rolled onto my side to watch the two men couple and had Sam leaning over on my side and whispered to me, 'Is that the same way that you fucked Peter?' she asked.

'Near enough, though it was on a bed and not on sand,' I told her.

'You mean he was able to take your cock up his ass like they are doing, as big as it is?' she said in awe at what she was seeing.

'Yes, and he enjoyed it,' I said in reply, me then starting to get another erection at the thought of fucking him again, his ass being tighter than Sam's vagina.

'Will….will you fuck him when we are back home?' she asked.

'Well I might if he asked me, but not at night though. He is your brother and needs sex as much as we do, so why should he go without. Not having anyone else to help him out in his need,' I said. 'You already know that I did before we got married.'

'But you're mine now,' she cried. 'What…er, would…er, I often wondered, er, what, er, how two men do it together. Would…er, do you think I could see how it's done with him?' she asked, not really knowing that it was almost the same as what those two men were doing near us, her really blushing now.

'I can only ask him, though I'm not sure if he will say yes. But there again, he might say yes if he's allowed to see us have sex, you know, quid pro quo,' I told her.

This gave her food for thought and the matter was then dropped but came to be a reality a month later.

In the meantime, our holiday came to a close after our two weeks of sun, sea, sand and sex and said our farewells to the staff of Lyon's Island and instead of the plane, took the boat back to Nassau. We spent that last day going round the shops and markets to buy things to take back home as presents, after which, we boarded the same plane that had brought us out and again I had the flying bedroom to sleep and have sex with Sam in there. So we joined the Mile high Club again before sleeping for most of the trip back home after having had a really wonderful honeymoon.

We took off from Nassau at five p.m. and had dinner before we took over the flying bedroom to have sex before falling asleep. With it being an eight hour flight, by Bahamas time, it was one a.m. but because of the time difference, the time in England was six a.m.

I had to speak to several taxi drivers about our destination and it was only the fourth one that agreed to the journey and considering the time it would take before he could return to the airport, it was quite a high sum of money that he wanted. But what the hell, we wouldn't be doing this again for a long time, so agreed. So three hours later, after having reached the town and then giving him directions, we arrived at the yard.

The day's trucks had already departed and we were greeted by Graham, Michael, Sheila, Katie and Peter with it quickly being known that we had arrived. I paid off the taxi driver and after he had left was greeted by a kiss from the females and a hand shake from the males, though Peter had given his lips a lick, would rather have kissed me, but he didn't.

'Look at you!' Graham had cried, giving Sam a kiss in welcome. 'As brown as a berry. All over?' he grinned.

'From top to bottom dad,' she replied with a laugh. I didn't catch all of the questions being asked as they were all trying to speak at the same time. It wasn't until we were inside the house did things become more coherent, and we were then able to give sensible answers to the questions asked. Some we prevaricated on, which I'm sure you can guess what they were.

Overall, it was a lovely welcome for me as I was now a member of the family and it was much appreciated. All through lunch, Sam gushed about how fantastic the honeymoon was, like being on a desert island with all that sea, sun and sand. She left out the sex part, though they guessed we had made pigs of ourselves with this. They were all delighted too, to be given the presents we had bought for each of them. After we had eaten, Graham went back to his office as did Michael, I wandered out into the yard with Peter, leaving the girls to talk among themselves.

'I've missed you Eddie,' Peter said as we walked round what was now my domain, being on a par with both Michael and Peter, now a family member. 'I wish I could have been on that island with you. Can we go to the toilets, I've been needing you so much?'

'I missed you too Peter, yes,' I said and followed him to the toilets which were close to the offices and went inside. Into one of the two cubicles we went, where, when the door was shut, we kissed each other and I had his hand rubbing the front of my trousers, feeling that with just being there with him, all alone, I had gotten a massive hard on knowing that I was going to fuck him. He got the front of my trousers open and pulled out my cock and pushed me to sit down on the pan. He then was quick to get his trousers off and turned round for me to see his bare bum as he lowered himself down onto my erection that I held upright for him to sit on.

What a pleasure it was to feel his ass widening as he sat on my cock, it slowly moving up inside the tightness until it was fully inside him as he was then sitting on my thighs.

'God, I needed this,' he said in a low and panting voice, as he began to move up and down on me. I held his waist in my hands as he moved, loving the tightness of his ass as he fucked himself on my cock and gave out little squeals of delight as he felt my cum beginning to coat his inside channel. It was only with me saying that if he got up off of me, I would suck on his hard erection that I was then rubbing in my hand, for he would have sat down on me for the rest of the day, flexing his muscle round my cock.

It seemed to be with reluctance that he slowly rose up, feeling my cock leaving his backside until I was out of him and he turned round for me to them take the head of his throbbing cock into my mouth and began to suck and tease the head as his hands came up either side of my head. I had to put a hand round his cock to stop him from actually choking me as he face fucked me. He'd really been saving himself for me for it seemed to be the most cum he'd ever giving me in my mouth for some even ran down my chin there was so much of it. I managed to swallow what I held in my mouth, loving the way it slid down to my stomach before he pulled out. I then stood up and had him lick his own cum off my chin before kissing me with his wet lips.

As he put his trousers back on, I got out of the cubicle and quickly washed my cock at one of the basins before putting it back inside my trousers, and with us both dressed properly again, went back out into the yard.

The following day, it was him sitting on the pan and me having his cock up my ass, loving the feel of his pulsating cock inside me and as I bounced myself up and down on him, just loved to feel his cum coating my insides. After lifting myself up off of him, having enjoyed having him fuck me, gave him my cock to suck and take in my cum to swallow with pleasure. That became our pattern two days a week to fuck and be fucked in the toilets, out of sight of everyone whilst we had the pleasure we gave each other.

But I've jumped ahead of myself with my telling you of what we did in the future though there's more to come. (Pun unintentional.)

After dinner, Sam said she was tired from such a long day and wanted to be excused to go to bed. I then said the same, getting knowing smiles from them all, and went upstairs with Sam into what was now our bedroom and quickly got undressed and into bed.

'As much as I loved that flying mattress, it's nice to be back in my own bed with my new husband,' she sighed as she rolled over to me for us to kiss.

With us kissing, my hand was fondling and moulding a tit, making the nipple rise up for me to then move down and suck on it, also giving it little nips with my teeth. There wasn't any objections either with me kissing my way down over her stomach and sticking my tongue into her pussy. I didn't stay down there long enough to give her an orgasm for I was feeling tired in spite of having slept on the plane, I had a massive hard on that needed seeing to and so moved up her body having my cock enter where my tongue had just been.

'Oh Eddie,' she sighed as I filled her. 'No sky to look at tonight.'

'Looking at you is far better,' I said, both of us smiling as I moved in my fucking of her and managed to hang on as she began to buck beneath me in the throes of her orgasm and give her my cum at the same time. I stayed laying on top of her until I felt my cock start to deflate before pulling out to a big sigh from her, and rolled over onto my back, but she seemed too tired to go down on me and only gave me a kiss before we both fell asleep.

IT WAS now back to the working routine with the alarm clock going off at half past six that morning, waking us up to have a shower and get dressed. No time for sex as breakfast was at seven with the day's work starting at eight.

I was in the office with Michael as the drivers started arriving for their truck keys and collect their orders for the day's work, getting ribald comments about my now being back from my honeymoon.

There was little for me to do with all the drivers having shown up, so I cleaned up the yard and straightened out the tool room that had become a bit messy with me being away. I also went and had sex with Peter which you already know what we did there in the toilet.

Graham had gone off for a two-week holiday with his mistress, leaving Michael in charge of the firm, and with him not being at home, there was less chance of us being found at what we did in the toilets

That night in bed with Sam and after having fucked and sucked her and her sucking on me, she came out with the question she had asked me before.

So finally one night, a shy Peter came into our bedroom. I could see that he really didn't want us to have sex with her watching and broke this down by kissing him, clearly in sight of Sam watching us. I got him to take my clothes off and then be naked, my cock, hard and upright as I moved in closer to take off his clothes, kissing both nipples when his shirt was off and also having a suck on his cock once that was free from his trousers. Sam moved over to one side of the bed for both of us to get on, our cocks swaying about as we did so.

We didn't go into the sixty-nine position for I had to save my cum for later, but went down and began sucking on his rampant cock, loving having it in my mouth, getting another thrill at knowing that Sam was watching me as I sucked and chewed on him. When he neared his peak, I lifted my head up off of him, but kept my mouth close to the head as I worked my hand on the shaft so that Sam could see the first spurt of his cum shoot out of the head into my open mouth and then for me to quickly take him inside to catch the rest without the losing of his cum that filled my mouth.

When he'd finished bucking his hips, with me now having my mouth full of his cum, lifted my head up and let Sam see the cum I had caught before swallowing it and then going back down to finish off my sucking of him.

Peter seemed to be reluctant to move for Sam to watch him being fucked by me, but I managed to get him to roll over and up onto his knees. Before I got between his legs, I got him to give me some sucking of the head of my cock, telling him to coat it with his saliva to give it some lubrication. This he did with a wide-eyed Sam watching.

After a few sucks and the head of my cock now glistening in the light, I got between Peter's legs and had Sam move down the bed to watch as I slowly pushed my cock up into his ass.

'Wow!' she said as the head of my cock got inside to be followed by the rest of me until my hips were tight up to the cheeks of his bum. 'I didn't think it was going to fit.' I couldn't see, but Peter told me later that he was sure his face had turned a bright red in letting her see me sticking my cock up his ass.

But with me now fully inside him, I began my slow movement of moving myself back and forth inside him until I knew that I wasn't far off cumming and began to move faster, ramming my cock in and out of him till I held him close up to my thighs as I began shooting my load up into his ass, having him give out little cries of delight as I sprayed and coated his insides.

I couldn't see then, but did a few minutes later, that with me cumming inside him, he had gotten another erection. It was only after I had pulled out to sit on my heels and he fell onto his side, did I see that his cock was up hard and lying on his stomach. So to finish off this display of two males having sex, I went down and sucked on his rampant cock till he came in my mouth and let her see me swallow it before getting off the bed to go and wash myself at the basin.

TIME PASSED. Graham was back and Michael and Sheila went off for a two week holiday, Sam then having to help Katie in the kitchen to see to our meals.

August arrived along with Sam and myself having our birthday on the same day, which was celebrated at a restaurant in town, with us now being twenty-four years old. It wasn't until we were in bed and me fucking her that she told me her little bit of news.

'I've stopped taking the pill, Eddie. I want to start our family. You said that this was the month to start for our child to be born next May,' she said, which was true.

Even though I didn't really want to start having children so early into our marriage, I wasn't going to spite myself by not having sex with her, so it was up to nature as to her conceiving.

Epilogue

As I have already mentioned, Steve had been driving back and forth to Germany and it was four months before he had a tyre go flat. He knew that he had got one for it was shown in the way the truck handled. He was on one of the Autobahns of Germany, way between two exits, and so pulled over onto the hard shoulder and with both indicators flashing, got out a triangle to set up further back along the road, got our new jack out of is brackets and set the machine in motion.

It proved its worth by him then being able to change the wheel in a short space of time before being able to continue his return to England where the tyre was then changed for a new one.

It was in September that Sam missed her monthly period and then knew that she was pregnant. Graham was as delighted as we both were, for him, it would be his first grandchild as Michael and Sheila, even being married for two and a half years now, hadn't as yet had a child, though not to be outdone, Sheila became pregnant two months later. This delighted Graham once again as there going to be a second grandchild. Sam and I didn't want to know what the sex of our child would be, waiting till the birth, though Sheila we heard, having had a scan, would be having a daughter.

May came round and that was when Sam went into labour. We'd phoned for an ambulance after her waters had broken and I went with her in this ambulance to the hospital, Graham and Peter following in a car. And so, on the fifth of May, I became the father of a lovely boy. Sam looked weary when I was allowed to see her with the baby in her arms and kiss both of them, thanking heaven that everything had gone smoothly.

He was duly christened two months later and with him being the first of the family, he was named as Adam Edward May.

Sheila had her daughter born two months after Adam and with us beginning our family with the letter A, followed suit, and she was christened with the name of Alice.

It was in September again that Sam told me she was pregnant again and as she had wanted, we had another son delivered in May, two days different from Adam. He was christened with the name of Barry Arthur May, later to be known as Bam.

It was when Sam announced that she was to have her third child that Graham went and had an extension built onto the house for Sheila was also pregnant again and what with having us now breeding like rabbits, the house needed more rooms. Ours was a daughter this time where Sheila then had a son. We carried on this alphabetical naming of the children and Sheila and Michael finished up with three children whereas Sam and I finished up with five, drawing the line now as they were enough for Sam now having outdone her father in the number of children sired.

Peter and Katie never did get married and were happy enough to be Uncle and Aunt to the children of the household which was a happy one. I still didn't manage to get Peter pregnant, though not from the want of trying in our weekly session of having sex as well as our monthly one with Sam watching when we did so.

As I've said, we were a happy household and it looked like it was going to be so for many years to cum.

THE END

Here is a sample from another story you may enjoy:

Amy Redek

Foxhole
Vixen of my Dreams
Erotic Bisexual Romance

IF I had asserted myself at the very beginning of my marriage, I would not be in the state of finding myself.

It would be better if I laid it all down along the line. You would see where I went wrong and used a phrase that fitted the bill, and that "Hindsight is the best viewing platform."

My name is Raymond Fox. I came from a middle class family based in Southampton. That's where my parents live and where I was brought up and educated until I went to a University to take up major in mathematics and banking systems. As a child, I showed a remarkable aptitude for numbers and it was suggested that my future should be in the Stock Market.

But even though the money to be made on the floor was quite substantial, if one was lucky, it could also be a bubble that eventually would burst with those who chose this route if they didn't get out in time. I had my sights on more of a long term position in the banking world, not making as much money, but a steady progression to doing so from such a stable profession.

I earned my master's degree at twenty one and was lucky to obtain a position with Charter's Bank, a local branch in Southampton, at the lowest position and worked there for eight years, slowly moving up until I was offered a position of Assistant Manager at a branch in Oxford. It was at my last interview that I met the Chairman of Charter's Bank, Sir Eugene Charter, the fifth member of this family whose great, great grandfather had founded this banking empire in the city. I came to get very close to him later as you will see.

He was the senior member of the board of five who were present at this interview, me being one of the last four being asked a series of questions about banking and my aims within the company. It lasted just over an hour and it was a really serious occasion with the astute questions being asked and it wasn't until a week later that I was summoned to the Head Office and told that I could now take over the management of their bank in Windsor.

My parents were delighted at this news even though I no longer lived in Southampton having moved out to lodgings in Oxford until now, and it was time to look for somewhere to live in the Windsor area. Not being a strong man in terms of my physique or in any other way except in the banking world, this position of manager really only required a quick mind in all the aspects of this profession, the handling of money and knowledge in the placing of it in the right places to make even more for the bank and its customers.

I did well there and got on with the staff under my control and it was a happy atmosphere and a pleasure to be working with such an amiable work force. I had been there for nearly a year when I received my invitation to attend an annual dinner of all the managers of the branches from all over the U.K. This was to be held at the Cumberland Hotel in Park Lane, London.

Suitably attired in my dinner suit, I attended and was just one of over a hundred other managers, some with their wives as well as the members of the company's board of directors. It was not only to hear speeches of how the bank was doing financially and a dinner but also there would be dancing, for which I silently thanked my mother in teaching me at an early age at how to conduct myself in the art of being able to dance well.

On entering the ballroom, I was greeted by Sir Eugene and after shaking his hand, was introduced to his wife, Lady Elizabeth whose hand I took and gallantly kissed the back of it as one did in the presence of royalty or persons of a higher standing. She smiled back at me and gave a short curtsey and introduced me to her daughter, Vivienne whose hand I took and kissed too, getting a deeper curtsey and an even bigger smile. Little did I know of her mind and even to this day, known as little now as I did then.

The dinner itself was excellent and I was very embarrassed at a part of the speech from Sir Eugene when he called out my name, asking me to stand as he presented me to all those gathered there saying that I was now the youngest and newest member of our bank. There was a lot of clapping of hands and with a very red face, gave a small bow in acknowledgement before sitting down to receive congratulations from those sitting at the same table as myself.

With the meal and speeches over, we were invited to move through to the ballroom for the dancing, where there were many small tables set around the floor with a large one at the far end which was for the directors and their wives to sit at during these dances. As people settled down at any other table, I was beckoned over by Sir Eugene.

'Well young man,' he began. 'As our newest and youngest manager, we are giving you the honour to open the dancing with Lady Elizabeth.'

I felt my face redden at this and saw the smiles on the faces of the others seated at the table. There was nothing I could do but offer my arm to Lady Elizabeth and escort her out onto the floor and with a bow to her as she curtsied, the musicians started to play and we began the waltz to begin the dancing. After a turn around the floor, others started to join in and was soon filled with other men waltzing their partners.

Again, I silently thanked my mother at being able to dance without putting a foot wrong and at the end, escorted her back to the table and invited their daughter, Vivienne for the next dance. This was a quick step and I'm sure she deliberately moved her leg tight in between mine at every turn and sure she felt the reaction at me having this beautiful young woman in my arms. I even had her quite large breasts press up close to me which caused me some confusion at knowing she could feel the erection I had inside my trousers at this close bodily contact.

She sweetly smiled at me at the end of the dance, her eyes shining and it was rather erotic to see the way the tip of her tongue moved over her lips in a brief sweeping motion before I escorted her back to her table. I was glad to sit down and take a big gulp of my drink and hoped that I could sit out the next dance until I had deflated somewhat.

It did and I danced with several other ladies at my table and in between, couldn't ignore the beckoning finger of Vivienne for me to go over and have another dance with her with the same result to my body. In fact, I had four dances with her all told and I knew that her method of dancing with me was deliberate, just to arouse me for her own amusement to see and feel my discomfort.

If you enjoyed this sample then look for **Foxhole**.

Also by this Author

The Painted Sword

Cruise Control

Wild Pleasures

Lending My Beloved

Lady of Cuckolds

Lady of Pleasure

Lady Magenta

Sexually Overdosed

Meeting My Fancy Dear

Prison Sex Slave

Chasing A Shadow

The Hostel

The Island

Thirst for Drugs and Pleasure

Forgotten Identity

Grey Memories

Chronos: Time Machine

The Hard Bomber

Honeymoon Abduction

The Yacht Sins

About the Author

George Eliot was a famous writer, though at the time, only male authors were recognised. It was in fact the pen name of Mary Ann Evans, a female.

When I started writing, I thought that if a woman could use a male name, why, with me being male, why couldn't I use the name of a female? Though to be different, I made my writer's name from an anagram of my real name.

I wasn't the brightest spark in my school days and it was only while being in the Merchant Navy did I self-educate myself. That being mostly literature, classical music and artists, like Tolstoy, Chopin and Rembrandt. After leaving the navy, I had several jobs, finishing up by being a working boss using my own maxim that 'Management is the art of delegation.'

It's when I became self-employed that I began to write, though sadly, not many of my books can be published because of certain laws that forbid certain aspects of life. This never fazed me for I was really writing just to please myself having a wide range of the human psych.

Having written ninety stories, my only aim now is to reach one hundred. I give thanks to the publishers for at least putting some of my efforts out for others to enjoy as much as I did in the writing of them.

From the Author

Check my page on Amazon and my blog for Updates and interesting info.

Author Central – http://www.amazon.com/Amy-Redek/e/B00A48NQ72
Author Blog – http://amy-redek.awesomeauthors.org/

If you enjoyed any of my books then please share the love and click like on my books in Amazon.

If you write me a review and send me an email I will send you a free book, or many.
(Just know that these emails are filtered by my publisher.)

Good news is always welcome.

One Last Thing, For Kindle Readers...

When you turn the page, Kindle will give you the opportunity to rate this book and share your thoughts on Facebook and Twitter. If you enjoyed my writings, would you please take a few seconds to let your friends know about it? Because... when they enjoy they will be grateful to you and so will I.

Thank You!

Amy Redek
amy_redek@awesomeauthors.org